Lithium

Elise Noble

Published by Undercover Publishing Limited

Copyright © 2017 Elise Noble

v5

ISBN: 978-1-910954-41-6

Edited by Amanda Ann Larson

Cover art by Abigail Sins

www.undercover-publishing.com

www.elise-noble.com

To Ben & Jerry.

CHAPTER 1

I TURNED THE bar of soap over and over in my hands, working up a lather. The sticky remains of Raspberry Ripple clung to my fingers, stubbornly refusing to shift under the weak stream of water.

The low purr of a car on the street outside sent me scurrying to the front window, but the shiny SUV crawled past the row of McMansions without stopping. A mom lost on her way to a kid's birthday party? A nosey realtor? I headed back to the bathroom and finished up, depressed by the woman staring back at me in the mirror. The last couple of weeks had taken their toll—with little sleep and the stress that came with every job, I'd developed eyebags and a fucking wrinkle.

The water ran clean at last, and I dried my hands on my fancy slacks. I needed to hurry. Not only was my vehicle bound to be reported stolen soon, but Ripple's wife would be home from Pilates at four. When she arrived, she'd find his pasty white body lying out on the bed, dick carefully arranged in his hand. At least he'd died happy. I wanted to be well clear of the place when her screams rocked the neighbourhood.

Chocolate.
Strawberry.
Mint Choc Chip.
Rum 'n' Raisin.

Peach Melba.

Pistachio.

What do you think of when you see that list? Hot summer days? Relaxing on the beach or by the pool, maybe? Two scoops in a cone, floppy sun hats, the smell of saltwater hanging in the air?

I envy you.

For me, that list meant three years of blood, sweat, and finally tears. And now I'd added another flavour to it—Raspberry Ripple, the latest victim of the Ice Cream Project.

What, I hear you ask, is the Ice Cream Project? Well, in American society, men exist who do things they shouldn't. Things that would make the public spit their cornflakes across the breakfast table and lock up their kids if they ever found out about them. Rich men, powerful men, who for one reason or another, weren't practical or cost effective to prosecute. So what did the government do? Hired me to take care of the problem without any comebacks or complications. An assassin. Fight fire with fire and all that. I got paid to melt them.

Take Ripple, for example—a corrupt police chief who'd gotten away with taking bribes for years unchecked, because the time and effort it would have taken to gather evidence and remove him outweighed the benefits. At least, until he took a backhander from a businessman known to hang out with kiddies in his spare time, and my employers decided enough was enough.

Since I started working on the project, I hadn't been able to touch ice cream. Even the sight of the stuff on a restaurant menu made me queasy. And Vanilla was the worst, plain old fucking Vanilla, my nemesis.

As I put miles between me and the house where Ripple's body lay, a little of the stress that had built up inside me while I planned and executed the job dissipated. Each time, that stress got worse. At thirty years old, I had the experience to kill quickly, cleanly, and creatively, but I no longer had the hunger, especially for dessert.

By the time I found a cheap motel, a dingy, squat little box within spitting distance of the freeway, the local newscaster crackling out of the radio in my "borrowed" Honda was busy warning his listeners about the dangers of too much fried chicken. So they hadn't found the body yet—a cop dead from a heart attack in the middle of self-induced passion would sure as fuck take precedence over counting calories in your chicken nuggets.

Which gave me the gift of time.

I shoved the door to my room open with my shoulder when it got stuck halfway, then clicked the light on. Home, sweet home, at least for one night. The place looked like a thousand others—a tired bed sagging in the middle, carpet that you wouldn't want to walk on barefoot, and a bathroom shared with four cockroaches and a moth. I peered at the kettle. The frayed wires invited me to play a game of Russian roulette with electrocution if I wanted a coffee.

I dumped my bag on the bed, then flung my itchy wig after it. Blonde had never been my colour. With the dark skin I'd inherited from an Indian grandmother, peroxide blonde made me look less exotic and more like a porn star. At least, that was what the police chief had said when he jacked off over my tits. His yellowed smile hadn't left his face even as he breathed his last, so I guess I'd done something right.

After twenty-six hours awake, I flopped back on the bed, desperate for a few hours' sleep before I moved on. Although where to, I hadn't quite decided. It wasn't like I'd put down roots anywhere. Since leaving home at the age of sixteen, I'd lived in eight different countries and travelled to three times that number. The longest I'd voluntarily stayed in one place was the four months I spent with Vanilla and look where that got me.

No, I was destined to be a nomad.

My phone rang as I contemplated a shower, weighing up the need to rinse off the sweat with the orange-tinged water dribbling out of the faucet. I shut it off and answered.

"You okay?" a woman's voice asked.

"Define okay."

"Well, I can hear you're alive, so let's go for satisfied with your work."

"It's done."

"Good. At least the Ice Cream Man might stop moaning for a day or two."

"More like an hour or two, if I'm lucky."

"What's next?"

"I don't know." I sighed. "I mean, I know what should be next, but... I'm tired, Emmy."

"Take a break for a week or two. Recharge."

"Maybe." A tropical garden somewhere, a hammock, a book, a cocktail menu. Loneliness. Boredom.

"Why don't you come here?"

"Virginia?"

"Or one of our other places. Pick one."

It had been a long time since I'd stayed with Emmy. Before Ripple. Before Vanilla. Her house was always full, and right now I didn't feel like being social, but nor did I relish the thought of isolation.

"How many people are there?"

"Me. My husband. Bradley and the other staff. Tia's moved to New York, so she's not around. I'll keep things quiet."

"In that case, I'll stop by for a few days." Aware that I sounded like I was doing her the favour rather than the other way around, I added a soft, "Thanks."

"You're always welcome, you know that."

"I'll see you soon." I did the calculations in my head. "Thursday."

"Thursday," she repeated softly, then clicked off.

Now all I had to do was "borrow" another car, switch my identity, find something to eat that wasn't fried chicken, and get to Virginia.

Easy.

CHAPTER 2

FIVE DAYS LATER, I laid out next to Emmy's indoor pool as she stroked up and down, barely making a splash. I'd shifted the sun lounger right back to the wall, but even then, it was too close to the water for my comfort. A couple of palm trees cast their shadows over me, their leaves blowing gently in the breeze from the fan heaters near the ceiling. Last time I was here, Bradley had installed a fake beach in the corner and the sand got in everything, but that was gone, replaced by a fucking ice cream kiosk.

I pretended to read a book, or rather a gun catalogue, but I barely saw the array of shiny barrels in front of me. Instead, I counted Emmy's lengths from the corner of my eye, and when she'd swum a mile, she stopped next to me and propped her elbows on the edge of the pool.

"Sure you don't want to join me?"

I shook my head quickly. Too quickly. Emmy knew what was running through my mind, and she climbed out and dragged another lounger up beside me.

"You still haven't been in the water, have you?"

"Does the shower count?"

She stared at me.

"Okay, fine. No, I haven't. You try nearly drowning and then see if you feel like going for a swim."

"You used to love it."

"I used to love a lot of things that turned out not to be so good for me."

"Jack Daniels?"

A bark of laughter escaped. "Him too."

Emmy reached over and squeezed my hand, reminding me of the downside of having a friend like her. She saw my pain while everyone else believed in my smile.

"So, what are you gonna do?"

"About Vanilla?" Of course about Vanilla, but asking the question stalled for time.

"The job still needs to be done."

I stared at the ceiling, sunlight twinkling through the glass and reflecting off the leaves of the miniature rainforest. "Did you get rid of the birds?"

"They were shitting everywhere. Stop changing the subject."

"I know I should deal with him, but the thought of seeing him again makes me want to curl into a ball and hide under my duvet."

"We all have moments like that."

"But we don't all fall in love with the man we're hired to kill." There, I said it. My failure as an assassin laid bare.

"True, although if my husband leaves bits of gun everywhere in the bedroom again, I'll be tempted to kill the man I fell in love with. Sorry. I'll be serious. Look, you made a mistake, and Vanilla is kinda hot."

Yeah. That was my downfall. Until the first night with him, sex had meant nothing to me. After my daddy fucked the soul out of me as a child, the act took on all the passion of a business transaction. I'd lie back while a man pounded away on top, thinking about the best way of achieving my objective, which in my case wasn't an orgasm, it was usually death. Oh sure, I'd moan in the right places, but out of practice rather than enjoyment.

Since high school, I'd known there was something wrong with me when it came to sex. While my classmates were chasing boys and experimenting with them behind the bleachers, I'd already been there, done that, and collected the mental scars to prove it. Instead, I waited until my daddy passed out, then snuck his gun out to the woods to practise. I loved the woods, and I loved that old Colt. I'd taken it with me when he died of heart failure—that and my battered copy of *Grimm's Fairy Tales* were the only reminders of my childhood I wanted to keep.

After my deep and meaningful relationship with a semi-automatic I tried dating, but men didn't do it for me. Eventually, I'd suspected I might be gay, but a little research showed that wasn't the case. An undercover job had led to a few nights spent with Emmy, who'd try anything once, and we both soon realised the girl-girl thing wasn't for us. Not permanently, anyway. Luckily, we came out of it with a friendship that lasted longer than any president, and over the years we'd had the occasional bit of...fun? Experimentation? Call it what you like. She was crazily in love with her husband now, and he seemed to view our antics with amusement rather than jealousy.

Although months could pass without us speaking to each other, when Emmy and I did meet, we picked up where we'd left off, and it was her I'd called after Vanilla did his worst.

Ah, Vanilla.

"He's a walking bunch of pheromones stuffed into a made-to-measure suit," I said wistfully. Not to mention the only man ever to make me come.

When it happened, when those elusive shivers of pleasure rushed through me, it was like an epiphany. Some women got addicted to alcohol, some got addicted to drugs. Me? I got addicted to a giant prick. And when I say giant, I'm talking about the man's ego and not his equipment. That was average at best.

"There's not many things that look better on a guy than a good suit."

"He wasn't bad out of it, either. Dammit! I have to stop thinking like this. He's an asshole. A murdering asshole." With dark, wavy hair, a chiselled jaw, and eyes that sucked you in until you felt breathless. Even now, my brain flip-flopped between wanting to put a bullet in his brain and wanting to put his cock in my mouth. He'd screwed me in every way possible—mind, body, and soul. "Maybe I could get some pills to help."

Emmy looked at me sharply, then rolled off her own sun lounger and squashed onto mine. "Honey, you are still taking your pills, aren't you? Tell me you didn't stop?"

"The lithium? Yes, Mom."

I might have had a few tiny issues. And by "issues," I mean that I was probably bipolar. And by "probably," I mean that I'd never been professionally diagnosed— the last thing I wanted was someone poking and prodding, not at my body and definitely not at my mind —but the symptoms seemed to fit. The lowest lows that sent me spiralling into darkness, followed by highs that left me grinning all day long. Pills helped. I'd been self-medicating for half my life. Now I was powered by lithium, kind of like a battery. Well, by lithium, bad memories, and crazy ideas.

When Emmy had picked me up in the early hours half a year ago, I'd been a gibbering wreck. A dark period had followed, but she'd given me some undercover work to take my mind off Vanilla, and these days...these days I felt okay. Okay-ish.

"Good. The lithium keeps you steady."

"You know me—like the Energizer Bunny, I just keep going and going and going. And by pills, I meant I should get something to kill my libido. It's taken on a life of its own."

"What happened with Raspberry Ripple? Did he have the same effect as Vanilla?"

"Fuck, no. I was going through my grocery list while he screwed me. The most exciting part was the air embolism I gave him at the end."

And that was what made me so good at my job. When the CIA had needed a girl to run honey traps a decade ago, I'd volunteered for the position and made it into an art form. Quite literally—I'd done it in positions that put the *Kama Sutra* to shame. Then I'd gone freelance and turned the art into cash. And until Vanilla, I'd never felt the slightest attraction to any of my targets.

"So, it's just Vanilla. Maybe you could try replacing him with a better flavour?"

"No more fucking ice cream."

"How about something different? Sticky toffee pudding? Cookie dough? Brownie? I know plenty of guys."

"I don't want another man. All they do is fuck up

your life and your sanity. I just wish I could go back to how things were, but the bastard's still alive, and I can't move on until I deal with that."

Emmy squeezed my hand. "Do you want me to deal with it for you?"

A lump came into my throat. At times like this, you really found out who your friends were. "Thanks for offering, but it's something I need to do myself. Closure and all that."

"The offer still stands if you change your mind."

I hugged her and she squeezed me back, and for the first time in months, I felt a thread of happiness. Why hadn't I come here sooner? We stayed like that until a shadow loomed over us.

"Should I be worried?" her husband asked.

She grinned up at him, then licked my face. I groped her breast as he shook his head, a slight smile creasing his lips.

"Not sure I'll ever understand you two, but if by any chance you want to help me try..."

Emmy let out a peal of laughter. "You couldn't handle both of us."

He leaned down, close enough that his chest brushed against me, and his musky scent invaded my nostrils. A perfect example of the male physique, good genes enhanced by hours in the gym.

"Try me," he whispered.

Emmy's pupils dilated and her right nipple hardened under my hand. I knew exactly what she wanted. But I felt...nothing. Nothing. A man like Black should have had me drooling. What the hell was wrong with me?

CHAPTER 3

AFTER MY TALK with Emmy, I knew I had to sort out the Vanilla problem so I could get on with my life. I'd start first thing tomorrow morning. After I'd used the gym. And had breakfast. And sorted out my laundry.

No! I'd start now. The ridiculously expensive Gucci timepiece Vanilla had bought me said it was half past seven. I stared at the watch for a few seconds longer, then unbuckled it and hurled it against the wall. The sound of the glass cracking wasn't as satisfying as I'd hoped.

Embarrassed that I'd lost control, I scooped up the jagged remains, tossed them in the trash, then went downstairs.

Emmy and her husband were the majority shareholders in Blackwood Security, a firm they'd started fifteen years ago and grown into a global player through hard work and possibly a few of Black's shadowy connections. While the public face of the company offered executive protection, training, technology solutions, and investigations, behind-the-scenes Emmy and a few others provided services similar to my own.

They'd offered me the use of whatever resources I needed, including the backup control room at their opulent home, and that was where I headed. As I walked in, Daniela di Grassi rushed up and threw her arms around me. She'd been one of Emmy's best friends for as long as I'd known her, and that made Dan a friend of mine too.

"How are you? It's been what, five months?"

Five months, two dead bodies, and a whole lot of sleepless nights trying to forget a man who I should hate. "Yeah, about that. I'm okay. You?"

"Neck's a bit stiff." She worked her head from side to side. "And my new Mustang's two feet shorter than it should be."

I stopped my eye roll halfway through and went for sympathy. "Aw, another car broken? What happened?"

"Dude I was chasing lost control on a bend and spun into me."

"And how's he?"

"Eating through a tube. Emmy said you needed some help locating Raul Barone?"

I grimaced at the sound of his name. "Figured it was time I did something about him."

"I can't believe you've left it so long. If he'd done to me what he did to you, I'd have shot his bollocks off ages ago."

If they'd been anyone else's bollocks, I would have. Although I preferred to use a knife. The intimacy of a blade up close somehow added to the horror. With a gun, one blast and it was all over.

A sigh escaped my lips. "I don't know why I haven't. Everything's messed up in my head."

"Love and hate are the closest emotions, and you've drawn that line a little wonky. One day it'll straighten itself out."

"As long as I end up on the right side of it," I

muttered.

"We'll all be here to give you a shove if you don't. Now, I've got good news, bad news, and worse news."

"Give me the good first."

"I tracked down Raul."

That was what I wanted, right? So why did a pit of dread open up in my stomach? "Where? Atlanta?" That was where he lived, where he and his family ruled their part of the city, untouchable. "What's the bad news?"

"He's on vacation. Well, it seems to be more of an extended trip."

"Where?"

"On his yacht."

Fuck. Water, water everywhere. "Where's it moored?"

Raul may have owned the yacht as a status symbol, and he enjoyed hosting parties on it, but I happened to know he got seasick if he spent more than a couple of hours on the open water. On one trip, he'd dashed from our bed six times in the middle of the night to puke over the side. No, he'd be anchored up somewhere, enjoying the nightlife.

"Right now?" She tapped a few buttons on the screen in front of us and zoomed in. "Grand Cayman."

Sun, sea, and money. Figured. His family had to launder their cash somewhere, and what better place to do it than one of the world's biggest tax havens? I peered at the picture Dan had called up. "Wow, the resolution on that's amazing."

"Emmy got it. I'm not sure how. There's a rumour floating around that she invested in a satellite company."

In front of me, Raul knelt on the sun deck, his tan

showing he'd spent quite a bit of time up there. He needed a haircut. But that wasn't my main concern. My jaw dropped as I recognised the brunette beneath him, her mouth open in a sigh as he massaged her ample tits.

"That's his fucking secretary. The one he hired just before he dumped me."

And when I said dumped, I meant it literally. You may wonder why I got so upset about the revelation that Raul was a cheating bastard when my attempted murder left me numb. Well, to me, murder was business. Trading me in for a different model was personal.

"She won't be doing a lot of typing in that position."

"That bastard! He told me she had a big mouth and it drove him crazy."

Dan clicked on the next photo, which showed Raul on his back, shorts around his knees as the brunette crouched over him. "I don't think he was lying."

When Raul told me it was over, I'd asked if there was another woman, and he'd looked me square in the eye when he answered, "There's nobody else, Sadie."

Dan flicked to the next picture in the series, with the woman leaning to the side so Raul could unsnap her bikini top. Dammit! He'd been a better liar than me.

"I need a gun and a plane ticket."

An arm snaked around my waist. "Have you finally seen the light?" Emmy asked.

I pointed at the screen. "He cheated on me. With his secretary. He couldn't even be original."

Emmy leaned forward. "He has no taste. Those are definitely fake."

"She's had her lips done as well."

"Ick. I always wondered what that would feel like. Do you reckon they go tingly?" She caught my glare. "Okay, okay. So, now what?"

"I'm going to finish my damn job."

"On the yacht? You know that thing sits on water?"

I gritted my teeth. "He has to come ashore sometime."

"Why not wait until he comes back to the States? Have you even been to the Caymans before?"

"Once." I didn't want to mention it was only for two days. "And at least it'll be sunny."

I motioned at the windows where rain fell in sheets from a leaden sky. Grey, like my fucking soul.

"I suppose he'll be off his home turf as well."

"And he won't be expecting me."

"Well, of course not. He thinks you're dead." She sighed. "If you're set on this, I'll give Bradley a call. He can give you a new look. Unless you plan on haunting Vanilla to death."

"Now, if I could induce a heart attack..."

"I was thinking more of a poltergeist. Do they throw knives?"

"They do now."

By nine o'clock, Bradley was fussing around the bathroom, muttering about split ends. "Who did this to you? It looks like a rat chewed it."

"Uh, a salon in Atlanta. It looked okay six months ago."

He threw his hands up and gasped. "Six months?

You've left it six months?"

"I had other things on my mind."

"Didn't you look in a mirror?"

"The whole point of my job is to stay out of sight. It doesn't matter if I don't look runway ready." Although when I lived with Vanilla, I went to the hair salon every two weeks, had my nails done each Monday afternoon, and never, ever ventured out without lipstick.

He sucked in a breath. "Well, I'm going to have to take a few inches off."

"Whatever. I don't care."

While he snipped and covered my hair with gunk, I busied myself reading the intelligence files Dan had sent over. According to his credit card statement, Vanilla took his secretary out for dinner at least four times a week, and from the prices, they were living on lobster and caviar. I looked back farther, to the months when we were together, and found he ate out five times a week when he only ever took me out three. That sneaky little shit! He must have been cosying up to her, even then.

"All done," Bradley announced, and I looked up.

Lesson number one. Don't ever, ever give Bradley free reign to do what he wants. "Where the fuck is my hair?"

He pointed to a messy pile on the tiled floor. "Looks fantastic, doesn't it?"

My waist-length hair was now a choppy bob, with a long fringe sweeping sideways just above my eyes. I'd worn it honey blonde with Vanilla, and in a fit of anger, I'd dyed it dark brown in my bathroom after he dumped me. Now it had cherry red overtones that caught the light as I flicked my head.

"It's different," Emmy said.

"Good different or bad different."

"I'd better say good while you're in reach of the scissors."

"It's Bradley I want to kill."

He took a couple of steps towards the door. "I just need to check on something."

As he sprinted along the hallway, I turned back to Emmy. "Maybe I should drink a bottle of wine and go to bed."

"Don't think like that. You still look beautiful. New hair, new start."

"I hope you're right."

CHAPTER 4

IT ALL SOUNDED so simple in theory—hop on a plane, travel to Grand Cayman, top up my tan, then dispatch my ex to hell.

"Are you sure you wouldn't be better waiting a week or two?" Emmy asked. "We could come up with an actual plan."

"It'll be fine. I've done this plenty of times."

"But not with the emotional involvement."

"Or the whole water-issue thing," Dan chipped in.

I stuffed another pair of shorts in my case and stood up, trying to work the kinks of a sleepless night out of my back. "I'll stick to the middle part of the island. It's not all boats and beaches out there."

"And how will you watch Raul's yacht from the middle of the island?"

"Uh, binoculars?"

Truthfully? I hadn't thought that far ahead.

"If you wait a week, I could come with you," Emmy offered. "I've got a couple of meetings coming up that I can't get out of, but I can shuffle things round after that."

"This is my mess. I created it, so I'll clear it up."

I caught the looks they gave each other and knew what they thought of that idea, but neither of them said anything. "Could one of you give me a ride to the airport?"

Emmy did the honours, thankfully. The way Dan drove, I'd have gone to the Caymans via the emergency room. As it was, we arrived almost on time, having hit a slight delay when Emmy got pulled over for speeding. Again. I'd once asked her how she still had a licence and she just laughed.

"I'll grab a coffee before I head back." She yawned wide, remembering at the last second to cover her mouth with her hand. "I've been up since five."

I planned to sleep on the plane. "Decaf for me."

Except we'd barely gotten into Dulles airport when we hit the first snag. "Where did all these people come from?"

The lines for security were almost out of the door.

A cleaner hovering nearby filled us in. "Security scare, miss. Someone phoned in a threat."

"Fuck it," I muttered under my breath.

Emmy knew exactly what I was thinking and trailed me out to the car so I could remove the disassembled bits of handgun from my luggage. On any other day, I'd have sneaked it through, but who knew what would happen if the rubber glove brigade decided to earn their money?

"Still sure you don't want to delay this?"

"I'll find a gun out there if I need one."

The truth was, I felt afraid that if I didn't go now, I never would. I'd put it off for long enough already, and while the anger pumping through my veins gave me the impetus to get on the plane today, who knew if I'd feel the same way after I slept on it for another night? When I woke up this morning, I'd already had second thoughts. It was now or never, and I hurried back inside the airport before I could change my mind.

"Don't think I've got time for a drink now," I said.

If anything, the line had grown longer while we'd been outside, a depressing snake of disgruntled travellers shuffling forwards a foot at a time.

"I'll save a bottle of champagne for when you get back."

At least someone had confidence in me. I gave her a long hug. "Keep it chilled."

"Of course. Call me if you need anything."

With that, I joined the happy throng and reached the gate just as my flight was boarding. As I'd left it to the last minute, the window seats were all booked, and I'd had to settle for the aisle. The lady next to me smiled as I sat down. Not many ninety year olds could carry off hot pink lipstick, but she was working it with the orange warm-up suit and yellow sneakers.

"Work or pleasure, hun?" she asked.

Well, it definitely wasn't pleasure, but I could hardly admit to it being work. "I just thought I could do with a week in the sun, and perhaps catch up with an old friend."

"I'm off to visit my family. My son moved out to Grand Cayman five years back, and now I've got three beautiful granddaughters. Would you like to see a picture?"

No. "Sure."

When she said picture, she meant album. Soon, I'd been treated to her entire life history, illustrated in glorious Technicolor. "And this is Maisie again. She wore that crocodile costume for Halloween—nearly gave the neighbours a heart attack, my son said. Look, here's one from a different angle. You can really see the teeth."

I glanced to my left, eyeing up the drinks cart slowly inching its way along the aisle towards me. Nearly there... Nearly...

The flight attendant gave me a perky smile. "Would you like—?"

"Vodka and coke. Don't worry about the ice. Actually, make that two."

Beside me, my new friend tutted. "Alcohol isn't good for you, hun. My friend Barb, she was always fond of a tipple, but now she's in hospital with liver disease. Gone all yellow, she has."

I snatched the little bottles from the hostess and emptied one into a plastic cup, topping it up with coke before I slugged it back. Why had I left my damn gun behind?

"Then her husband fell down the stairs after a Knights of Columbus meeting and broke his leg in three places. The hospital gave them adjoining rooms, but there was nobody at home to look after their cat so Mabel along the road took it in, but Blackie didn't get along with her dog, and Coochie Benson heard the fight three doors up. The place looked like a massacre afterwards, so Mabel said, and now they're arguing over who'll pay the veterinarian."

Had she even taken a breath in that? I looked at my watch—still two and a half hours to go. I reached for the other vodka, but we hit turbulence and it fell off the tray table, rolling away under the seat in front.

"Goddammit."

She shook her head and wagged a finger. "You shouldn't take the Lord's name in vain, young lady. My neighbour's son used to blaspheme morning, noon, and night, and he got run over by a truck outside the Chick-fil-A on the corner of Fifth and Eleventh. The Lord moves in mysterious ways."

The man in front reached through the gap in the seats with my bottle of vodka in his hand. "Should have ordered a third," he whispered.

Even that wouldn't have cut it. I'd be hearing her in my sleep. Hmm... Sleep. I knocked back the bottle, then rummaged in my carry-on luggage.

"Say, is that a bird out there?" I pointed at the sky. "I didn't think they flew this high."

My new friend peered out the tiny window long enough for me to dump a couple of Ambien into her coffee and give it a quick stir. I hated taking them myself, but I knew they'd come in handy for something. She was soon snoring peacefully beside me, and I lay my own head back to get some rest.

Only it didn't quite work out that way. As soon as I closed my eyes, Vanilla came to visit. This wasn't an infrequent occurrence, but why wouldn't my subconscious mind let me relive the good parts of our relationship? Our cosy dinners. The way he used to massage my shoulders after a long day. The hot sex.

No, I only ever dreamed about one thing. The day he tried to kill me...

I couldn't complain about the morning. What girl wouldn't be happy with an orgasm followed by a lazy brunch? And the afternoon wasn't too bad, although if I was honest, the number of spa days he sent me on was wearing a little thin. Even the evening started off okay.

A glass of wine, followed by sex—he didn't perform quite as well as he usually did, but I'd still give him an eight. Then it happened.

"You have a meeting?" I asked.

He'd shot his load, pulled out, rolled over, and got up.

"Something like that."

"Is there a problem? Will you be back tonight?"

"I don't know."

"Is everything all right?" A "meeting" wasn't unusual at that time of night, but his cold demeanour rang alarm bells.

"Fine."

Was the male version of "fine" anything like the women's? "What's happened? Something's wrong, isn't it?"

He finished tying his shoelaces, then straightened up. "Here's the thing. I don't think we should see each other anymore."

The heat drained out of my body. It was the oddest sensation. First, the tips of my ears cooled, then the chill continued downwards until my toes went icy. I was left kneeling on the bed, gasping like a fish breathing its last. "What?"

"We had a good time, but with work and everything, I need some space."

The bastard was dumping me? No, no, no. This wasn't how things were supposed to work. The plan was that I'd seduce him, then steal the secrets of his family's organised crime empire, and then weep convincingly when had a terrible accident. At no point did I get kicked out of his bed like a cheap hooker.

"So you fucked me, and now you're leaving?"

He shrugged. "You seemed to enjoy it."

My first thought was for the knife in my purse. I could slice his balls off, one at a time, and... No. It wasn't worth getting arrested for murder. I'd managed to avoid that over the years, and I didn't want my first night in a police cell to be one where my face was streaked with mascara as I cried over being such a complete fucking idiot.

Instead, I narrowed my eyes at him. "Is there someone else? Is that what it is?" Hell, my voice sounded like I was channelling a banshee.

"There's nobody else, Sadie. Like I said, I just need some time to myself. This isn't working anymore." He shrugged into his jacket and strode towards the door. "Vadim will drive you home."

He stepped out, and I heard mutterings from the hallway. Clearly Vadim was being instructed not to let me trash the place or steal his boss's beloved Rolex collection. I glanced over at the dresser where they normally sat lined up in a row—seven watches for seven days. They were missing. The son of a bitch had really thought this through, hadn't he?

At that point, work was the last thing on my mind. I'd never been in that situation before. I ditched my dates, usually at the morgue or occasionally jail if I was feeling generous, not the other way around. Apart from Emmy, the only genuine relationship I'd had that lasted longer than a week ended when we drifted apart. After two months, he'd wanted to spend nights with his buddies, while I preferred heartfelt conversations with my Glock.

And Raul had the gall to screw me over, quite literally, then break my heart. It had taken me a while to lend it out to him, and he repaid the favour by taking a knife to both ventricles. Chest tight, I snatched up my clothes, tugging my dress over my head with a carelessness that popped a string of sewn-on beads all over the floor. They skittered away along with my sanity. Damn that man! I needed to get out of this room, away from the shame of what he'd just done to me.

Which was why I walked right into his trap.

When I opened the bedroom door, Vadim glowered at me—his default expression. Not a word passed his lips although I didn't think I imagined the tiny smirk as I got up close. Head held high, I marched towards him, aiming for the front door. Raul said Vadim would take me home, but I'd call a cab. I didn't want to spend a second more of my life near that steroid-ridden asshole.

Except I didn't get a choice. As I strode past Vadim, the sting in my thigh made me jump, and it took a few agonising seconds for me to register the syringe sticking out of my leg.

"What the...?" I never finished, not the thought or the sentence, before Vadim faded to black and gravity called me home.

Cold air bit at my face as I rejoined the world. Something was stuffed in my mouth, and when I tried to take it out, I found I couldn't move my hands. With my feet bound as well, I could only mumble as Vadim and another of Raul's henchmen hauled me out of the trunk of the car.

My hair whipped around my face as the wind caught it, stinging my eyes. By rubbing my face on my shoulder, I managed to get the gag out, and I was about to scream when I looked around and realised the futility. I didn't recognise where we were, but darkness stretched along the road in either direction. The absence of traffic noise told me nobody would be coming to help. Indeed, the only sound other than the wind was the rushing of water under the bridge Vadim had parked on.

As my senses returned, I knew what was about to happen. The concrete block my ankles were tied to acted as a bit of a giveaway there. For a second I considered begging for my life but quickly remembered who I'd be talking to. No sense in giving Vadim the satisfaction.

Instead, I looked up from my position slumped on the tarmac and asked, "Why?"

Had I gotten careless and blown my cover? If so, what had given me away?

Vadim shrugged. "Boss has found this is the easiest way of dealing with break-ups. No hassle. No complications."

Behind him, the other guy mimicked, "Oh, Raul, I love you so much. Please give me another chance. I'll do anything. Even..."

Vadim gave the man a look and his words trailed off. "Boss doesn't like when women get clingy."

Complications? Was I clingy? I'd always been bemused by every woman who needed a man to complete her, so how had I turned into one of them without noticing? I hadn't had time to work out where I'd gone wrong when Vadim picked me up again. His associate lifted the block, and without so much as a sayonara they heaved me over the bridge parapet.

I'd been groggy from the drugs before, but the fall stirred my senses, and I gulped in a ragged lungful of air before I hit the water. The near freezing temperature jerked me awake as the concrete block sucked me down, down, down. Think, Fia, think! My heart threatened to break out of my ribcage as I bent myself backwards to feel what I was dealing with. Some sort of twine, tied to a pair of handcuffs biting into my ankles.

The black waters swirled like a vortex of hell as I tugged my knees towards my chest. I couldn't see the bottom, but I knew I'd only have seconds to get my hands in front of me before I landed in a silty grave. Luckily, I'd practised a hundred times in the gym, making my shoulders scream and my wrists burn as I contorted my hands over my head. I'd just managed that feat when my concrete anchor dug into the sludge, holding my feet steady as I bobbed around in the current. Liquid ice fought with the hot panic in my veins as I willed myself to stay calm, although at that moment, a heart attack seemed preferable to drowning. My pulse steadied a fraction as my willpower won out over stone-cold fear. How long did I have left? Thirty seconds? Forty?

Something touched my lip, a kiss in the dark, and I reached up and clutched at my necklace. *My necklace.* It saved my life that night. A gift from Emmy for my birthday a few years ago, the abstract platinum design concealed a hidden handcuff key, and I used it to free my feet first. Another wave of terror rushed through me as the tugging river caused the rope to tighten. My lungs were close to bursting when I finally undid the lock, and I barely had the energy to kick to the surface. One mouthful of air, and I tumbled over and over in the turbulent water, fighting to free my hands. Finally, I got them loose too.

Breathe, Fia. Breathe.

The river swept me along, swollen after a week of near-constant rain, taking me away from the eyes of Vadim and his cohort. I caught a glimpse of them up on the bridge, illuminated by their car headlights, facing the opposite direction as they watched the spot where they'd thrown me in. Too bad I'd come out downstream.

My arms hung limp at my sides as I floated with the current, too tired to paddle. It was only when I saw the lights of a small town ahead that I summoned my last reserves and stroked towards the bank. Beer cans and plastic bags littered the beach I landed on, and for ten, twenty, thirty minutes I lay there, tossed out by Raul, at home with the trash. For a moment I'd considered sliding back into the water and sucking in a lungful, but the determination that had got me out of my hometown and onto my future career path stopped me. I'd come too far to end it that way. Then I began shivering, and the danger of hypothermia became very real. So, I did the only thing I could—staggered to my feet, broke into an empty house, and called Emmy.

CHAPTER 5

WHEN THE PLANE landed smoothly at Owen Roberts International Airport, the old lady next to me was still snoring away. Still, it could have been worse. She could have been in the aisle seat. As it was, I slipped out before the cabin crew tried to wake her.

According to Dan, Raul was anchored up at the Cayman Islands Yacht Club in Governors Creek. So much for my plan of sticking to the centre of the island. The yacht club lay to the west, in the midst of meandering waterways. I wouldn't be able to go half a mile in any direction without hitting the wet stuff. On the positive side, the number of tourists in that area would make it easier to hide. Maybe I'd even find the time to top up my tan?

Without knowing how long Raul planned to stay, I avoided any long-term commitments and used the internet to find a cheap apartment I could rent by the week. I didn't want a hotel—the idea of housekeeping poking around in my room made me cringe.

"Four hundred US dollars a week," the apartment owner said when I asked about the price. Not that I cared about the money. When I killed Vanilla, I'd get my usual fee plus a bonus for completing the list. Oh, and a deep sense of satisfaction, don't forget that.

"Four hundred?" I repeated.

"You won't find anything cheaper."

That was what worried me. We'd met in a café, and the guy's shifty eyes focused anywhere but on me as promises of air conditioning, a modern kitchen, and a king-size bed flowed from his lips. But not only did he take cash, the second-floor, one-bed unit was hidden away on a side street and didn't have a sea view—a definite plus point.

"I'll take it."

The key came on a dismal piece of orange string, and his hand-drawn map led me to the wrong street to start with, but eventually I found 102 Seaview Gardens, a misnomer on both counts, and let myself in.

Okay, I'd stayed in worse places but not by much. The dust on the air conditioning vents said they hadn't been used in years, and the bed was a small double at best. My lovely kitchen? As long as I didn't want to do anything but microwave, I was good to go.

The luxury I'd left behind at Emmy's taunted me. What was I doing here? Oh yeah, I was supposed to have murder on my mind. Except right now, all I wanted to do was sleep.

The door of the closet creaked ominously when I went to hang my clothes up, and then the handle fell off. Wonderful. Was that a sign of things to come? I stuffed the selection of bikinis Bradley had insisted I bring onto a shelf, then lay back on the lumpy bed.

Where should I start?

The answer was, I started with yoga. For months after my near-death I'd neglected myself, but when I couldn't do my jeans up anymore, I'd forced myself back into an exercise routine.

Every morning, I rolled out of bed and onto the yoga mat beside it. I'd tried everything over the years, but the ancient art built strength, stamina and flexibility like no other. Before the sun rose, I'd worked through a selection of poses, the asanas, finishing with a few minutes of squats, burpees, and crunches.

Then it was time to run. The dingy concrete stairway outside my temporary home brought me out in a filthy alley. I skirted a dumpster and headed for civilisation, with a vague plan to learn the layout of the neighbourhood. Sure, I'd checked it out on a satellite image, but there was nothing like a poke around on foot to understand a place's character.

My route took me past homes and stores, getting prettier the closer to the edge of the island I got. Then the water caught my eye as the morning light glistened off its ripples. Too soon. Too soon for that. Time to head back.

When I closed the door of the apartment behind me, disappointment set in. How could I have come to this? I used to love the water. In Vietnam, I'd spent three months living in a hut on the beach, for crying out loud. Every morning I swam, in the afternoons I dived, and when I wasn't in the sea, I was on it, sailing or surfing. I'd even gone spear fishing to catch dinner.

Sweat dripped from my brow, and I forced myself into the shower. After I'd shampooed my hair, I did it again, just so I'd have to stay under the tepid water for longer.

I needed to get over this crazy fear. Little steps, right?

When the water ran freezing, I stepped out and got dressed, then blow dried my hair. A huge pair of sunglasses completed my outfit. I set three goals for the afternoon: shop for essentials, organise transport, and walk to the sea.

At first, I planned to buy a car, but when I stopped at the tiny grocery store three blocks from Seaview Gardens, a tatty card on the noticeboard at the front of the store caught my eye.

For sale:
Aprilia 125cc motorcycle.
Eight years old but smooth runner.
Good price.

Only a moped, really, but a bike had advantages over a car—I'd avoid getting stuck in traffic and it was easier to hide. Oh, and no one would bat an eyelid if I wore a helmet. Hiding my face from Vadim's beady eyes would certainly be an advantage.

By four, I was the proud owner of a slightly dented scooter, and even better, the guy took cash. Sasha, my alter ego, didn't like the idea of leaving a paper trail, so that was perfect. I parked my new set of wheels up behind the apartment, thankful the seller had thrown in a lock and chain for ten extra Cayman dollars.

Once I'd stacked my food into the woefully inadequate refrigerator, I headed for the sea. The tang of the salty air invaded my lungs long before I reached the water, and each breath made my heart stutter. I called on every ounce of willpower to push myself forwards. I'd once used mind over matter to survive days in the jungle, hostage drills, and thirty-mile runs over hilly terrain. Now I needed all that training for a simple walk along the coastal path. Oh, how I'd fallen.

One foot in front of the other. One step at a time. I forced myself along the sidewalk on trembling legs until I saw the sea in all its hideous beauty. I longed to turn and run back to my shitty apartment, but I forced myself to keep going. The sight of the water brought the memories back—the feeling of helplessness as the darkness closed over me, sinking to the bottom, struggling to breathe.

Five minutes. Just five minutes.

I counted down, glancing at my watch every ten seconds as I mentally unlocked the handcuffs, swam for my life, floated beneath the fucking bridge again. My heart pounded against my ribcage. But I stood there, twenty feet from the sand, watching the ebb and flow of the tide until I gave myself permission to retreat.

Five minutes. Tomorrow, I'd do ten.

It took me four days to get close enough to the harbour to see Raul's boat, *Liquidity*. The behemoth was moored up in a row of others, their owners vying for the crown of most ostentatious fucker on the island. With his gold-plated sun loungers, Raul was definitely in contention.

Fifteen minutes was all I could take, and that wasn't necessarily a bad thing. Any longer and I risked questions—some nosy prick would notice me hanging around and start interfering. I needed to come up with a plan, one that didn't involve pretending to be a tourist taking photos. The sightseeing thing would work for one day, maybe two, but any more and Vadim's sharp eyes would lock onto me.

I cut back to my dingy rental through side streets, keeping out of sight of the sea. Once I'd eaten a hasty lunch of fresh fruit and coffee, I dragged out my laptop. Before I left, Mack, a friend of Emmy's and Blackwood's resident computer guru, had installed custom encryption software that meant I could keep in touch with the team at Blackwood undetected. Usually on jobs, I was out on my own, and knowing I had the support of a team in case of emergencies made me feel a little better about being stuck on a damned island. But not much.

First, I fired off a quick message to Emmy, letting her know I hadn't died or lost my mind. A single word came back: *Good.*

Then I set about the task at hand—plotting and planning. I didn't need the fancy toys for the planning part—Google Earth did the trick nicely. I studied the area around the marina in detail, from the water itself to the streets radiating out beyond.

How could I spend all day at the marina, without touching the water itself, and remain unnoticed? For a brief moment, I considered getting a job at one of the stores that dotted the area, but having to work would be a distraction I didn't want for money I didn't need, and the application process would be a hazard in itself.

Then on the edge of the marina, set to the side of the strip of stores that made up the area's retail opportunities, I spotted a wide deck laid out with colourful chairs and cute little tables. Maybe, just maybe...

Monty's seafood restaurant was quiet when I walked in —only two tables were occupied, one by a couple and another in the corner by a solitary man reading the local newspaper. Good. That gave me hope.

A perky waitress bounced up to me, order pad in hand. "You want a table?"

"I was hoping you might have a seat free on your second-floor deck? A friend said the view was wonderful."

"Sure we do. And the view's great—you can see right across the marina from here."

Perfect.

The waitress—Miranda, according to her name badge—showed me to a lovely table looking out to the open sea. I pointed to a spot on the other side instead.

"Is there any chance I could sit there?"

"Of course, but it's not so pretty." Her quizzical expression said she didn't understand why I'd turn down her offer of the perfect blue horizon.

"I know, but I can see the harbour, and I like to watch the world go by."

She shrugged. "In that case, take a seat. We have a brunch menu being served right now, and lunch from twelve."

I held up my laptop bag. "Okay if I stay for both? I'm a writer, and I'd love to work here in peace for a couple of hours. My friend said great things about your coffee."

Miranda beamed at me. "Ooh, what are you writing? Am I allowed to ask?"

"Yes and no. It's a novel about a female assassin, but I'm ghostwriting so I can't tell you the name of it."

She clapped her hands together. "How exciting!

Absolutely, you can stay. Just let me know if you need a power cable—I'm sure we can sort something out."

I set my bag down, trying to hide my elation. "What do you recommend for breakfast?"

"The waffles taste great. We serve them with syrup and fresh cream."

"In that case, I'll have a portion of those and a black coffee."

My chosen table had bench seats each side, big enough for two people each and padded with lime green and turquoise cushions. Better still, it gave me a perfect view over the marina. A potted palm hid me from view, but I could easily see *Liquidity* through the gently swaying fronds, one boat from the end. Luckily the low catamaran in between us didn't impede my view of the deck. And the restaurant served waffles. Things were definitely looking up.

I adjusted my floppy straw hat and set up my laptop. With the sun behind me, I saw Raul's deckhand polishing the railings on the main deck in his black and gold uniform. Tacky. How did the boat and its marble fucking bar ever impress me? They say love is blind, and I sure proved that.

The cursor on my screen blinked, and I opened a blank document. Chapter one, page one. How did a person write a book, anyway? Fiction seemed dull compared to my life. Over the past decade, I'd been places and done things that would seem far-fetched in even the wildest of novels. Maybe I could start my autobiography? Even if someone did read it, they'd never believe it was true. As Mark Twain once said, truth is stranger than fiction. Yes, I'd put my life on paper with a little tweak or two. Good plan.

Decision made, I clicked on the screen and began to write.

I turned the bar of soap over and over in my hands, working up a lather. The sticky remains of Raspberry Ripple clung to my fingers, stubbornly refusing to shift...

CHAPTER 6

THE WAITRESS WASN'T kidding when she said the waffles tasted good. After living on food that didn't require cooking for the last few days, I savoured every mouthful. Except the last one. I wanted to throw up the last one.

Because as I took that final bite, Raul walked out of the salon with his bimbo-slash-secretary hanging onto his arm. I choked in disgust as she pressed her oversized breasts against him and rubbed his chest. What did she have that I didn't? Apart from double F-cups, obviously. I glanced down at my more modest Ds, hidden under a floral sundress. He'd never mentioned them being a problem when we were together, and he'd certainly sucked on them often enough.

Was it my personality? Had I not paid enough attention to him? Or had I given off weird vibes while I planned his ultimate death? I still couldn't understand where things had gone so wrong.

Oh, and look, for a full house there was Vadim. While I'd made the trip to take care of Raul, if I could make Vadim's life uncomfortable in the process, it would be an added bonus.

It would be easy to think I hated Vadim because he tried to kill me, and I can't deny that irked me a little. But on that evening, he was a professional doing his job, just like I had many times over. I'd have been a hypocrite if I based my assessment of his character on that little episode. No, I disliked him so much because he was a nasty person in general.

At first the little things annoyed me—he never smiled, never said thank you, never held a door open. I'm not old fashioned, but that's just basic manners. Even then, I might have written him off as a common asshole until the dog incident.

Raul's regular driver had succumbed to man flu, and he'd asked Vadim to step in, a request which pleased the miserable bastard no end. He'd slammed the car door behind us so hard it was a wonder it stayed on its hinges. As we drove back to Raul's penthouse, Vadim handled the limo with all the finesse of a cow doing gymnastics, and I surreptitiously checked we both had our seatbelts securely buckled.

"When's Mario back?" I whispered to Raul.

"Tomorrow. I don't care how sick he thinks he is."

With only a few blocks to go, I was in the midst of thanking German engineering for getting us there in one piece when a stray dog darted across the road in front of us, and Vadim swerved. Now, any normal person would have swerved away from the moth-eaten mongrel, but not Vadim. He aimed straight for the poor old soul, and when the wheels bumped over the dog's skinny body, Vadim's lips curved up in a sick grin.

The man simply enjoyed causing others pain, and that was the moment I vowed, one day, I'd make him suffer.

But not today, although he didn't look too comfortable in the heat. His beige suit jacket didn't fit in with the relaxed island lifestyle, but he needed it to hide his gun. As I watched, he settled back onto one of the loungers and picked up a newspaper. His posture didn't scream bodyguard—far from it—his crossed legs and slumped shoulders grumbled of boredom. At least he wasn't expecting trouble, which made my job easier.

Raul stripped off his polo shirt as he selected a seat opposite his bodyguard, and the secretary leaned over and locked lips with him. I had to look away. No matter how much I told myself I hated the man, it still hurt to see him with another woman.

Deep breaths. Count to ten.

Think. Plan.

I had a job to do. Raul's personal life didn't matter. I couldn't let it get in the way of work again.

"More coffee?" Miranda asked, jug in hand.

"Love some." Preferably with added Prozac.

As the afternoon wore on, I started getting down to business. First, I sketched out the parts of the boat I could see, and then I drew out a rough plan of the inside from memory. Just to be on the safe side, I asked Dan to obtain the plans for *Liquidity* from the manufacturer. I may have been on board half a dozen times, but mapping the locations of the seacocks had been the last thing on my mind. And if I got the urge to sink the boat, those little things were important.

Vadim left as I ordered lunch, jogging along the water's edge in shorts and a vest. He'd always maintained his fitness, and I harboured a suspicion there'd be steroids hidden away on the yacht. Nobody got that big the natural way. The second of Raul's bodyguards, a shorter guy I vaguely recognised, took Vadim's place on the deck as Raul carried his lunch to the table outside the salon.

As Raul fed his secretary something I couldn't quite identify from my lofty perch, I picked at my grilled tilapia. I'm sure it was delicious, but I'd lost my appetite. Maybe I should have ordered two plates of waffles instead?

Or possibly pancakes? I'd spotted those on the menu, lurking between the French toast and omelettes. I stole a glance at my stomach again, bulging slightly over my shorts. No, I needed to stick with the fish.

As the restaurant filled up, I jotted down notes under the guise of writing my book and stored everything on one of Blackwood's secure servers. Miranda stopped by every so often to check I was okay, but other than that, nothing disturbed me apart from the gentle lap of waves against the shore below.

Halfway through the afternoon, I became numb to the sound, cocooned amongst the colourful cushions and fragrant potted plants, and by the time I settled my bill and left for the day I felt more positive. For the first time since I'd set foot on the island, I began to think that maybe I could succeed. That perhaps my hare-brained trip to the Caymans wasn't such a crazy idea and I'd cross the final flavour off my list.

Then I could move to the desert and avoid ice cream for the rest of my life.

Each day, I refused to let myself near the waffles unless I'd walked a little closer to the water's edge. The day I actually dipped a toe in the sea, I added whipped cream. By the end of Sunday, six days later and with a liberal application of willpower, I'd paddled up to my ankles and I couldn't button my shorts anymore.

I'd also written pages of notes, and with Miranda's hourly questions about how my "book" was going, I'd made it as far as chapter two—a visit to my ex and a quick rehash of life with my daddy. I had no wish to dwell on that man any longer than I had to. Many times I wished my parents had dumped me on a doorstep at birth. That way, I'd have had a chance at a normal life. How would I have turned out if I'd graduated high school? Gone to college? Maybe I'd have settled down with a nice guy and never killed anybody at all.

And I'd never have met Raul. The slippery bastard had only left the yacht twice during the day, and I'd followed him to meetings at two different banks. The rest of the time he'd been holed up with her, the secretary, either on the sun deck or down below doing things I didn't want to think about.

Vadim went ashore more often—occasionally to pick up something at the store, and every afternoon to work out. I'd tailed him there once, but Bud's Gym was located in an ex-warehouse with high windows, and I'd stick out like a stripper in a choir if I tried going in there. The clientele ranged from muscle-bound to Incredible Hulk, and the only woman I saw go in was the colour of gravy browning and looked more like a man than ninety percent of the male population.

A few visitors showed up at *Liquidity* to break the tedium—a florist, a delivery from a local sushi place, and a courier carrying a small box. I made a note of the name on the van so I could ask Mack to take a look at the sender later. Hacking into the courier company's database would be a five-minute job for her.

But apart from that, all was quiet. I relaxed as best I

could, trying not to let my fear of the sea well up inside me.

Next week, I needed to step the surveillance up a notch—never an easy task alone but I'd had plenty of practice. Of course, on this job it would be more difficult than usual because even with my new hairstyle and a hat, one mistimed glance from Raul, Vadim, or the rest of their staff and my identity would be revealed. And in the evenings, I could hardly hide behind sunglasses.

Yes, the next phase of the Ice Cream Project required careful planning indeed.

CHAPTER 7

MONDAY MORNING, AND I had my day all planned out. Yoga. Go for a jog. Brunch at Monty's and hold the whipped cream. Then I was going on a boat trip. No, really. Miranda had told me about a glass-bottomed boat that did trips around the island, and I planned to be on the two o'clock sailing.

"If you don't get on that bloody boat, I'll fly over and throw you in the sea," Emmy had said to me when we spoke earlier. She'd called while I was still in bed, my back aching from the lumpy mattress.

For a second I was tempted to let her. I knew she'd come to the Caymans and help if I asked, but I needed to salvage what little pride I had left. "I love you too."

"I know. But seriously, how's it going?"

"Slowly. I just wish he'd get off the boat more often. That secretary must suck like a vacuum cleaner." I scored a bullseye with an apple core in the trash can. "It makes me feel so inadequate."

"Honey, you're great with your tongue. Raul has no taste."

"Why didn't I kill him when I was supposed to? I stalled for weeks, and all for the sake of a few orgasms."

"We all suffer from lapses in judgement sometimes. I mean, look at me and Luke."

Luke was her ex-boyfriend. Nice enough but dull by

Emmy's standards. "He didn't try to kill you."

"No, but he might have bored me to death eventually. You sure you don't want me to visit? Take your mind off things for a bit?"

"I can't. I've banned myself from anything fun until I get the nasty stuff done." Or I could stay in bed all day and ignore the world. Maybe just another hour... Stop it, S... What was my name again? Oh yeah, Sasha. "Has any more intelligence come in?"

"Raul's rented the berth at the marina for three more months, so it doesn't seem like he's leaving any time soon."

Great, so I didn't get much choice over the water. I'd been secretly hoping he'd get bored with island life and head back to Atlanta. Sure, his family would be a bitch to deal with, but I'd rather face Mafiosos with guns than the gentle waves.

But he was staying, and so was I. "Makes sense for him to be here. High season lasts until mid-April, so he'll probably go home before the hurricanes and heat start. Did Mack track down what arrived in that courier package?"

"You don't want to know. It's not important."

"Oh, just tell me, would you?"

Emmy gave a heavy sigh. "It came from Victoria's Secret."

"You were right. I didn't want to know." I wanted to grab Raul by the balls and twist them off. "Anything else?"

"Mack reckons he's laundering money through shell companies and funnelling the proceeds into offshore bank accounts. She's found two accounts so far, but from the amount of time he's spending in the Caymans, either there are a lot more or he's obsessed with his suntan."

And I knew how little time he'd spent outside. "So, you need me to find the numbers?"

"It would help. The Ice Cream Man might even crack a smile."

"I've only ever seen him look cheerful once, when Chocolate died in that avalanche."

"He never did like Chocolate."

But I did. In sauce form. On my waffles. "I need to get to work."

"Remember, tough times don't last, but tough people do. Take care of yourself."

"I will."

It wasn't as if I could trust a man to do it for me.

After a six-mile run, I suffered through a lukewarm shower and took my seat at Monty's. Miranda put a reserved sign on the table for me each morning now, just in case anybody else took a fancy to that spot. Today, the grey hue of the sky suggested rain on the way, and the air felt heavy and clammy. The thin jacket I'd brought wouldn't stand up to a downpour, and I kept my fingers crossed that the rain held off until after my boat trip. Water coming at me from both directions would be more than I could take.

"The usual?" Miranda asked.

"Could you bring a fresh fruit platter instead? I need to go easy on the calories."

She let fly with a peal of laughter. "If I ate as many waffles as you, they'd have to roll me home. How's the book?"

"Uh, yeah, it's going well."

After coffee, I scanned the marina as usual, but something bugged me, and not just the minuscule bikini the secretary insisted on wearing. What was it?

I took another look, more slowly this time, left to right. The old-timer sitting on a bollard at the edge of the quay, splicing a mooring rope. A couple of deckhands carrying crates of wine onto a yacht. The assistant in the souvenir store who came out for a cigarette every half hour on the dot. The waitress at the coffee place near *Liquidity*, who rivalled the Ice Cream Man in terms of happiness, scowling as she served a blond-haired man. Three teenagers...

Wait. Back-up. The blond-haired man. I'd seen him somewhere before. He wasn't overly familiar, but I recognised him. Where from?

I stared at the darkening clouds in the distance, thinking. Then it came to me. We'd been on the same flight over. He was the man who'd handed my vodka back when it rolled under the seat in front of mine. I relaxed a little, satisfied now I'd remembered.

Was he on vacation? Or here for work? Did it matter? I put him out of my mind as I ate a late breakfast, but at one, when I left for my boat trip, he was still there, staring out into the bay.

"Take my hand."

One of the crew reached for me across the gangplank of the Yellow Submarine, which may have been the colour of a daffodil but definitely wasn't a sub.

I faltered on the jetty with a foot-wide plank of wood being all that stood between me and twenty feet of salty water. A fish darted through the crystal blue, not a care in the world.

"It's okay. I won't let you fall."

Logically, I knew I wouldn't drown. Even if my swimming skills deserted me, the guy on the boat would no doubt dive in and play the hero. Some women might even enjoy that, seeing as he was fairly easy on the eye. Light brown hair, suntan from working outside all day, sinewy arms. Cute. But still I hesitated.

His eyes twinkled. "You want me to carry you?"

No, I damn well did not. I gritted my teeth and danced across the plank, only breathing again when I touched the deck.

He grinned at me. "See, that wasn't as bad as you thought, was it?"

Yes. Yes, it was.

As if being on the water wasn't bad enough, passengers could climb down into the hull of the catamaran where glass panels gave a view of life under the water. Dread crawled up my spine at the mere thought. A group of children rushed past, laughing and jostling as I perched on a wooden bench on the outside deck, as near to the middle of the boat as possible.

A few minutes later, the engines rumbled into life, and we set off to sea. My buddy from the gangplank sauntered by, whistling, but I didn't share his joy. Cold sweat dripped down my back as we left the marina, and although the brochure promised a trip around the coastline, with every extra yard away from land we got, my heart beat faster. What if the boat sank? What if I fell over the railing? What if…?

"You okay?" my new friend asked.

"Define okay."

"You look like someone died."

Me, nearly. "I'm just not very keen on water."

His cap shadowed his face as he tilted his head. "Was a boat trip the best idea, then?"

"Nothing like facing your fears head on."

He patted my hand. "In that case, good going. What's next? Jet skiing?"

A shudder ran through me before I could stop it. "Not likely."

The guy chuckled. "You gonna go downstairs? There's some interesting fish in this part of the bay. Lionfish, giant puffers, even the occasional shark."

"Maybe later."

"Can I get you any refreshments? Something to drink?"

"You have vodka?"

"Only soft drinks, I'm afraid."

"In that case, I'll pass."

Ten minutes ticked by, then twenty. My phone pinged with an incoming message.

Emmy: You on the boat?

S: Yes, I'm on the fucking boat.

Emmy: Scuba next.

Yeah, right. If I survived the ride without having a heart attack, I'd seriously consider moving to the Sahara.

The first drops of rain fell as we turned around in the open sea, and I huddled under the roof that covered the front third of the deck as streams of water ran across the painted floor. The wind whipped up and blew the rain in sideways, and my hair flew in all directions. Everyone else disappeared down below.

Well, except one person.

"You don't want to hide from the storm?" gangplank guy asked.

"Not enough to brave the fish."

"I promise it's safe down there." He grinned as he took a seat next to me. "No piranhas, and the sharks have stayed away this week."

"I believe you, but I'm fine here."

"Look... What's your name?"

"Sasha."

"Look, Sasha. We don't like to leave guests up here on their own, and my hair's going all frizzy." He took off his cap and ruffled the ends of his crew cut, which couldn't have been more than half an inch long. "Take pity on a guy and let him go somewhere dry." He held out a hand. "Come on, what do you say?"

His fingers hovered an inch from mine, and when his eyes didn't leave me, I reached out and put my hand into his much larger one. His skin was dry to the touch whereas mine exuded a clamminess I only ever got when I was ill.

"That's better." He lowered his voice, which took on a husky tone. "I promise I won't let anything happen to you."

"What's your name? I don't even know your name."

"Brax."

I swallowed the bubble of fear rising in my throat. "Then let's go, Brax."

My heart pounded as he led me down a flight of steep stairs into the bowels of the boat. Excited chatter broke into my thoughts, chipping away at my fragile control.

"Look! A shark?"

"That's not a shark; it's a tuna."

"Hey! Did you see that? I swear it was a stingray."

Brax helped me onto a slatted wooden bench in the middle of the compartment.

"See, that wasn't so bad."

I stared at my lap, trying to pretend I was anywhere except on a boat, but the rocking motion gave it away. The child in me imagined the glass viewing windows cracking and the water rushing in, and...

Brax wrapped an arm around my shoulders. "What happened to make you so nervous around boats?"

"I fell out of my granddaddy's cabin cruiser when I was six and nearly drowned." Thankfully my lying skills hadn't fled in my hour of need.

"Ouch. I can see how that would put you off. Where did that happen?"

"Florida. My grandparents bought a condo down there when they retired."

"Well, while you're here, we'll get you used to the water again. You want to come out on the boat tomorrow?" He grinned, showing almost straight teeth. "I won't charge you."

Money was the least of my worries, but I appreciated the offer. "I'll think about it."

"Are you sure you don't want to look at the fish? Nothing I can do to tempt you?"

"No, I don't want to look at the fish."

He chuckled and pulled me closer, and out of the corner of my eye, I caught a dirty glare from the girl next to me. What was that for? Brax? Yeah, probably. Maybe I should have been flattered to have the attention of an obviously cute guy, even if it had come

about through me acting like a total lunatic.
    But as usual, I didn't feel anything.

CHAPTER 8

AS I EXPECTED, watching Raul in the evenings proved to be more difficult than in the day. I toyed with the idea of having dinner at Monty's, but as darkness fell, the place filled up with couples and I'd have stuck out sitting in the corner with my laptop. Even more so without it. What would the other diners think of me? The girl who'd been stood up? Or the one who couldn't get a date in the first place. Or worse, the woman on the prowl—I wasn't blind, and I knew I looked all right, which made hanging out alone an invitation for unwanted company.

So, for the last two evenings, I'd skulked in the shadows of the alley between the chandlery and the café, the dark purple hood of my sweater low over my eyes. A tipsy man ventured in, dick out for a piss, but he stopped mid-stream when he spotted me.

"What the fuuuuu—?"

I pointed at his shoe. "You're dribbling."

"Bitch."

Gee, thanks. I couldn't help chuckling as he tucked himself away and stumbled out of there, but the hairs on the back of my neck soon prickled as I saw movement on *Liquidity*.

Vadim marched down the gangplank, followed by Raul and the secretary, and I ran for my moped. Where were they going? Judging by the bimbo's attire—short skirt, big hair, dangly earrings—I guessed to dinner or a bar. Raul wore his usual suit—a black slim-fit accessorised with wingtips and a thin-lipped grin. What did I ever see in the man?

Thankfully, their taxi didn't drive fast, another symptom of the island vibe, and I tailed them to the buzzing streets of Seven Mile Beach and a not-so-classy-looking nightclub. Business or pleasure? Seeing as he'd never taken me out to any of his meetings, I doubted he'd want the airhead there either, so I guessed at pleasure.

Heavy bass pounded out of the door, and when the bouncer stood back, I saw the couple go down a flight of dark stairs leading to the basement. In my indigo jeans and hoodie, I wasn't in line with the dress code, so even if I'd wanted to, I couldn't have followed.

The doorman glanced in my direction, and I kicked the moped into gear. Dammit. No alleys and no dark corners to hide in meant a wasted evening. All I could do was return to my apartment, get some sleep, then try again tomorrow.

In the morning, the rain clouds had passed, and I took my now-customary place on the deck at Monty's. By the time I'd eaten breakfast and drafted a poor attempt at chapter three, Raul still hadn't appeared. Guess he'd stayed out late last night, getting his eardrums assaulted.

But I did see somebody else. The blond guy caught my attention as he waved at the surly waitress in the waterfront café. She poured him another coffee as he read the newspaper. Or at least, he pretended to. I caught him glancing over towards *Liquidity* on more than one occasion.

Was I imagining his interest? Could he be watching something else? Another boat? Birds on the horizon? A pretty girl?

Vadim stepped onto the platform at the stern, dressed in another ill-fitting suit, pale grey this time. Guess it wasn't easy to find a good tailor when one had the physique of a gorilla. He lowered the motorised gangplank and hopped onto the shore.

And the blond man tracked him as he walked to the café, bought a sandwich, and hustled back to the boat again. Too lazy to make his own lunch?

I'd worked out the routine on the boat by now—the chef worked from seven until ten, then came back in the evenings from five until nine. Flowers arrived every other morning, and the sushi arrived each day at three, with Vadim taking delivery. I suspected that would be Raul's lunch for the following day, or perhaps a snack. He'd always loved Japanese food and raved about its dietary benefits, although his obsession with his health didn't extend as far as the twenty a day he puffed his way through, and he rarely exercised. He claimed daily sex was quite enough, and I'd been stupid enough to go along with it.

Anyway, back to the blond. From that moment on, I split my attention between *Liquidity* and him, and there was definitely a connection. At every movement on the boat, the mystery man peered over his paper, his attention focused.

Who the fuck was he? And did he present a threat?

I wasn't worried about myself—he hadn't spotted me, and he wouldn't unless I wanted him to. But what did he want with Raul?

One thing was for sure, if he kept watching in such an obvious way, Vadim would ask him that question before I did. Vadim may have been a total asshole, but he wasn't stupid. In many ways, he was smarter than his boss.

That meant I needed to find out the mystery man's identity before he oh-so-mysteriously disappeared. Did Raul have any spare concrete blocks on board? I'd be surprised if the answer was no.

Right after lunch, I told Miranda I'd run out of ink in my red pen and headed into town. After a quick trip round the stores, I'd acquired three new hats, two pairs of sunglasses, and a top-of-the-range camera. The salesman proudly told me I'd be able to count the legs on a spider at a hundred yards, although I suspected he may have exaggerated slightly.

But it would be perfect for my purposes.

I changed into a different T-shirt, bright pink with a turquoise bird strutting across the front. Easy enough to remember, which may have seemed counterintuitive, but give it some thought: If anybody asked about me afterwards, would a person recall my face or the in-your-face outfit? That's right. They probably wouldn't even know my hair colour.

Then I slung the camera around my neck and headed for the marina. The Yellow Submarine would have to wait until tomorrow.

On my jaunt around the boats, I took a bunch of photos of *Liquidity*, a couple of a grumpy Vadim berating the deckhand for a mark on the gold railing around the bridge deck, and a nice selection of the blond. Oh, and about a hundred pictures of the sea, but I could delete all those as soon as I got back. I didn't need any more watery reminders.

"Can you find out who he is?" I asked Emmy when I made it back to my crappy room. "I don't know if he's important or not, but I don't want to take a chance of him getting in the way."

"I'll get Mack on it. And you're sure he was on the same flight?"

"Ninety percent."

"That makes life easier. We can start with the passenger manifest. Mack's getting her hair done right now, but we should have something with you by tonight."

"Thanks, babe."

For years, I'd worked on my own out of choice, since my days at the CIA, in fact. Their idea of teamwork meant putting the organisation first and everyone else second, which taught me the only person I could rely on was myself.

But I had to admit, I liked having Emmy's assistance. She'd asked me to work with her at Blackwood many times, and after six years out in the cold, I was approaching the point where I'd agree to it. When I finished the Ice Cream Project. I couldn't think straight until that was over.

My foot tapped of its own accord the next day as I waited on the dock for the Yellow Submarine to arrive. *Hurry up*. I needed to get this trip around the bay over with so I could get on with the rest of my day.

After ten minutes, the boat chugged back into its berth and satisfied day trippers streamed back onto dry land. I spotted Brax manning the gangplank again, and half a minute later he saw me too and glanced at his watch.

"Early today?"

Eleven o'clock—hardly dawn. "No sense in prolonging the agony."

He offered me his hand, and this time I took it as I crossed into the boat. "Are you gonna sit with the fish?"

I turned back, looking over my shoulder as I headed to the seating on the deck. "One step at a time."

It didn't take long for the boat to cast off again, and I blocked out the sound of the rushing water by thinking back to the conversation I'd had with Emmy before I left the apartment this morning. At least I knew who the mystery blond was now.

"Took us a while to track him down, seeing as he's not in the system. No priors, not even a speeding ticket. But Mack wrote some fancy new image recognition software and put it to good use."

"His name?"

"Leo Moore. Thirty-one years old. Six foot one and this time last year, 190 pounds."

"Did you find anything useful?"

"Oh, yeah. Are you ready for the pictures?"

"Hit me."

And she did. Seventeen emails worth of Mr. Moore in various stages of undress, all taut muscles and golden skin. I paused on one of his naked ass before I tore my eyes away from the screen.

"He's a model?"

"Fitness model. Although he doesn't seem to have done any shoots lately. Mack couldn't find anything since last year."

The shame of it. "So, what's he doing hanging around Raul?"

"Who knows? You're sure he's not just on holiday? Or working? Maybe he's come to the island for a shoot. You know, sun, sea, teeny swimming trunks."

I screwed my eyes up, trying to get rid of that image. "He's spent too much time at that café. What else did you find?"

Nobody went through life and didn't leave a trail.

"Mack's still looking, but we've got a big government job on at the moment. She's having to fit it in around that." Emmy sounded apologetic.

"I appreciate any help you can give."

"All we've got so far is that he used to own a gym in Atlanta, but it closed down six months ago. Money troubles. The bank foreclosed on the building."

"Atlanta. Same place as Raul."

"I don't usually believe in coincidences."

Neither did I.

Brax interrupted my musings by dropping into the seat beside me. "Come on, we're halfway round. The fish are getting lonely down there."

"I'm sure they'll manage without me."

"Okay, I'm getting lonely."

"I bet you're not short of female admirers."

"True." He sighed. "So, a forty year old just pinched my ass. Take pity on a guy, would ya?"

He'd used that line yesterday. But damn if I didn't want to. "Ah, now the truth comes out. Fine, I'll come downstairs, but if I see anything bigger than a trevally,

I'm out of there."

"Trevally? So you *do* know something about fish?"

Shit. I could hardly tell him I'd been qualified as a technical diver for the last decade, could I? I'd been down to a three hundred feet many times and seen a hell of a lot more than trevallies. Think enemy submarines and suspect boat hulls. But today I was supposed to be Sasha, hydrophobic since the age of six. All this water gave me brain fade.

"I think I saw a documentary on ocean life once."

Brax took my hand and tugged me gently away from my sanctuary. "Let's see what's out there."

We didn't see any trevallies, just a school of barracuda and a solitary southern stingray half-buried in sand at the bottom. Oh, and a pissed-off woman with skin like leather and a top that barely contained her assets.

"Is that the forty year old?" I whispered to Brax.

He nodded and grimaced. "We seem to get one of those every day."

The trip went faster than last time, and I felt a momentary burst of elation as the Yellow Submarine docked. I'd survived! Another whole hour surrounded by wet stuff and I hadn't been sick once.

Brax walked onto the shore with me. "Can I tempt you with one of our longer trips? We often see dolphins once we get farther out to sea."

"I'll have a think about it."

He smiled across at me, then reached out and squeezed my hand. "How about dinner? I finish at five, and I'd love to take you out for something to eat."

Dammit. Why did men always have to spoil things by asking me out? Brax was a nice man, but he certainly didn't make my heart beat faster, and no way was I going to screw up the Vanilla job with another pointless attempt at romance.

"My boyfriend probably wouldn't be too happy about that." I gave Brax a lopsided grin.

"You're taken? Figures. But you can't blame a guy for trying, eh?"

"Guess I can't."

"See you around, Sasha."

No, he wouldn't. "Bye, Brax."

CHAPTER 9

AFTER MY AWKWARD moment with Brax, I took comfort in familiarity.

"Waffles please, with whipped cream and a bowl of strawberries."

I worked on the offsetting principle. Emmy swore by it. The vitamins and shit in the strawberries more than made up for the waffles, and the cream contained calcium and was therefore healthy.

Miranda didn't bother to jot my order down. "And coffee?"

"You know me so well."

A quick glance over the balcony told me Leo was also in his place, reading a paperback with the remains of lunch on a plate in front of him. Today, he wore navy blue shorts and a white polo shirt, but I couldn't help reminiscing about the muscled ass I now knew lay underneath.

Whoops. No, I didn't reminisce. I didn't think about naked men, ever. Well, maybe Raul... I gave myself a mental slap. Not even Raul. I needed to stick to business.

And today that business meant following Leo back to wherever he was staying.

I'd gone through seven cups of coffee and risen halfway from my seat to go for a pee when he pushed his chair back. Dammit. Talk about timing. My bladder protested as I shoved my laptop into its case, threw a tip on the table for Miranda, and raced down the stairs. *Give me a break and don't let him be staying far away.* It would be just my luck if he decided to take the scenic route.

He didn't, but what he did was almost as bad. I lagged well behind as Leo walked to Seven Mile Beach and hopped on the yellow line bus, which started on its slow meander towards George Town. No hurry, no stress. The driver had all the time in the world. I was on the verge of hopping off to piss behind a bush when Leo disembarked two stops before the town and cut into a narrow side street. *Oh, please say he didn't have a long walk.*

For once, luck took my side. He stopped after a hundred yards, and compared to his apartment block, mine was a palace. Why had he chosen that place? Hiding out like me? I recalled Emmy's comments about foreclosure. Was he short of cash?

I paused on the street, head down as I crossed my legs and pretended to consult my phone. A minute after Leo walked through the outer door, his shadowy form passed a window on the second floor. Good—I knew where he lived now.

And thank fuck for that because I had more urgent matters to attend to. Like finding a bathroom.

"So, you're going to take a look at his place?" Emmy asked.

"Tomorrow."

"Mack found more pictures. Dan's pinned one of them up next to her computer and she's talking about flying out to help you."

I groaned. "Dan thinks with her vagina."

"I'll stop her, don't worry. Renting a stripper usually works for that. Anyway, we've started on Leo's background. His parents live in Kansas, but he doesn't seem close to them. No flights home, no phone calls. One sister, but she dropped off the planet a couple of years back and we haven't worked out what happened to her yet. Oh, and he's broke."

So, the apartment was out of necessity. "Figures. Any indication of a connection with Raul? Or Vadim?"

"Nothing yet. Maybe something to do with the gym? Didn't you reckon Raul was into a protection racket as a hobby?"

"Yeah. Hmm, it's possible. I'll let you know what I find here."

"Did you go on the boat again?"

"Yeah." I told her about Brax. "Why me?"

"Because you're pretty, honey. It's a blessing and a curse. When that thug broke your nose a few years ago, I had hope, but the doctor fixed you up too well."

I rubbed the bridge, the slight kink unnoticeable if you weren't looking for it. Emmy and I had gotten into a bar fight when some pervert pinched her ass, and my nose bled all over the pool table when some brute smashed me across the face with a pool cue. Hardly my finest hour, but at least I had the satisfaction of knowing he wouldn't father children.

"I suppose I should look on the bright side. If Raul had gotten his way, I'd have been a bloated corpse by now."

"True. So make sure you stay safe. Don't expect me to identify you in the morgue if you fuck things up. There are limits to our friendship."

"Thanks, babe. You always know how to make a girl feel good."

"Welcome. Talk soon."

The next morning, I tumbled out of bed at ten, tired from spending six pointless hours watching *Liquidity* the night before. Raul went to bed early while I didn't crawl in until the small hours.

"Why?" I groaned to myself. "Why do I do this?"

I mean, I could have retired—I had the money to. But that would mean quitting the Ice Cream Project, sacrificing my professional integrity, and giving up a $2 million-dollar bonus that could buy a hell of a lot of waffles.

And Raul would walk free.

No way was I letting that happen.

Not just because I wanted the bastard to suffer like I did, but because of the hundreds, maybe even thousands, of other people he inflicted his cruelty on back home in Atlanta. Drugs, prostitution, protection, illegal gambling—his family was into it all. Barone Senior had started the enterprise back in the sixties, and through a combination of luck and ruthlessness, they ruled the city's underworld. Now, they owned half the cops too, which meant the only way to remove them from power was to fight fire with a flaming inferno. Or with Snow. With Barone Senior getting on in years, the Ice Cream Man and his cohorts decided their best course of action would be to take out the heir elect: Raul.

Raul had inherited his father's mean streak as well as his penchant for breaking the law. Rumour had it he put two men in hospital last year just for looking at him funny when he showed up at a dive bar in his suit. And worse, on the night he watched as Vadim and his colleagues beat one of them into a coma, Raul left our fucking bed to do it. He was one cold bastard.

So, I took a cold shower to wake myself up, then bypassed Monty's in favour of a quick stroll past the café. Yep, Leo was there already. At least somebody got some sleep last night.

Twenty minutes later, I stood outside his apartment but not for long. The first man to walk through the communal door held it open for me as I patted my pockets to find my non-existent key.

"Thanks."

His eyes took a slow trip over my body, and I avoided the urge to punch him.

"No problem."

The guy gave me one last glance before he let himself into a first-floor apartment, and I strolled up to Leo's place, seemingly without a care in the world. But inside, I was buzzing. Work always did that to me, particularly when I was about to open a door without knowing what lay on the other side.

Leo's lock was a piece of shit. Child's play, literally. A simple pin tumbler of the type I'd been picking since I was a little girl and my daddy used to lock me in my bedroom. He never did catch me. Took me thirty seconds to get it open and half of that time was spent putting my gloves on.

Where did I start? Glancing round the single room, it was obvious Leo didn't plan to be here long term. The place made mine look luxurious. A bed, a table and chair, a door-less closet, and a grubby kitchenette—that was it. The tiny refrigerator in the corner contained enough food for a couple of days, all healthy crap, and only one shelf in the closet contained clothes. Shower gel and a razor graced the basin in the cupboard-sized bathroom. Was that everything he'd brought?

I kept a careful ear open as I searched the place more thoroughly, but on past form, he'd be at the marina all afternoon. Usually I took photos before I started to ensure I put everything back in its place, but the place was so empty there was no need.

He'd slipped an old laptop behind the bed and hidden his cash in the toilet tank like a complete amateur. The only find of any interest was a four-inch lock knife in a pocket of the jacket slung over the solitary wooden chair.

Why did he need that? Attack or defence?

He hadn't chosen a great weapon, if I were to be critical. A few drops of blood and his fingers would slip on the smooth wooden handle, and the fat blade wouldn't slip neatly between a man's ribs. No, he'd leave a mess with that one.

I tapped my leather-clad fingertips on the chipped table next to the microwave. What now? Did I go back to the marina and pick up a late lunch? Or should I stay and have a chat with Mr. Moore?

I had to admit, curiosity was eating away at me.

Knife in hand, I took a seat.

CHAPTER 10

DUSK CREPT ACROSS the island, lengthening the shadows on the floor as I waited. What did Leo think he was playing at, watching Raul? And why? What was he waiting for him to do?

My ass cheeks were numb from sitting, and I shifted on the wooden seat, trying to get comfortable. A splinter caught on my shorts. Oh, how I longed to stretch out on the bed and smooth my aching back. Where the hell was Leo? He'd never left the café this late before. Had he been spotted? Had Vadim got to him? Had—?

A key rattled in the lock, and I pulled my hood forward. Not so much that I couldn't see, but enough to hide my face. And I prepared to spring up if necessary. Leo's knife may have been in my pocket, but I couldn't be sure he didn't have another one.

A plastic bag crinkled as he dumped it on the scarred counter next to the sink. Ah. He'd been grocery shopping. More salad, probably.

I waited.

Then he turned.

"Who the hell are you?"

He froze midway between me and the door, eyeing his escape route and then turning back to size me up.

That was telling. He thought of running first. Not

such a tough guy. Me? If the roles had been reversed, Leo would have been on the floor by now, most probably unconscious.

"That doesn't matter right now. I'll be out of your way soon enough. I just stopped by to ask you a few questions."

"You're a woman?"

"No, I just have a really high-pitched voice. Yes, I'm a woman."

"But you've broken into my apartment."

"Stop being such a sexist pig. Just because I have breasts doesn't mean I don't know how to open a door."

"But it was locked."

"Or operate a set of lock picks."

He tried again. "Who are you?"

"Sit down. On the floor."

"Why?"

"Because I have your knife and I'm asking nicely."

His eyes widened, the light filtering in from outside catching on the whites. "How did you...?"

"Oh, just sit, would you? Otherwise we'll be here all night. I'm hungry and I'm already late for dinner, thanks to you taking your time."

"I'm not sure sitting down's a good idea with a knife-wielding maniac in my room."

He looked towards the door again and took a step in that direction.

"Oh, for fuck's sake, I'm not a maniac. I'm perfectly sane. If it makes you feel better, I'll put the knife down."

"Go on then."

He flinched as it whistled past, an inch from his ear, and embedded itself in the cupboard hanging on the wall behind him. I wasn't bothered—I already had my own knife in my hand, ready to follow if he made a wrong move.

"Sit."

He sat.

"Better. Now, tell me, why do you sit at the marina all day watching Raul Barone?"

"I don't know what you're talking about."

Oh, he did. That momentary hesitation before he answered? Dead giveaway. "Coffee, newspaper, grouchy waitress. Need any more reminders?"

"Maybe I'm just thirsty?"

"And maybe I'm a fairy princess. Will you answer the fucking question? We can dance around the truth all night, but I'm getting bored here."

He leaned his head down, eyes closed. "How did you know?"

"Because you're in plain sight all day and you look at the yacht every thirty seconds. And there's nothing in the Cayman Compass but puff pieces on local dignitaries, lost cats, and a whole bunch of ads."

"I didn't think I was that obvious."

"Trust me, you are."

"Wait—how do you know I'm there all day? Why are you watching me?"

I sighed. It was difficult to do this without giving a few snippets of information away. "Because I'm not watching you. I'm watching *Liquidity* too. I thought I'd better give you a friendly warning to back off before you get hurt. Raul's henchman doesn't mess around."

"Vadim?"

"Yes, Vadim."

"Why are you watching the boat?"

"Curiosity killed the cat. And the fitness model if he's not careful."

"You know who I am?"

"Yes, Leo, I know who you are. And if I know, you can be sure as shit Raul can find out too."

He sagged back against the wall, stretching his legs out in front of him. Not an easy position to come back from if I attacked. So, why had he chosen it? I suspected resignation combined with more than a touch of incompetence.

"I've not had much experience at this sneaking around stuff. I'll need to get better at it."

"No, you need to stop it altogether if you want to stay alive."

"I can't." He gave a shuddering sigh, and his voice took on a haunted tone. "I don't have anything left to live for, anyway."

Dramatic much? "Why? What happened?"

"Raul Barone killed my sister."

Of all the things he could have said, I hadn't been expecting that one. Raul murdered another girl? Why didn't I know that? I'd looked into his background thoroughly. Emmy had too. Was Leo playing me?

"He's never been charged with the murder of a girl, or even interviewed."

The only time he'd been accused of killing someone was when his business partner showed up with a bullet through his head. Even though the gun that fired it was registered to Raul, a good lawyer still got him off. Plus the rumours said he had cops in his pocket. One of the many reasons he'd found his way onto the Ice Cream Man's list.

"No, he never got charged, and the police didn't

believe me when I told them who did it. That's the whole problem."

"So how do you know it was him? How did he kill her?"

"Why should I say another word? What if you're working with him?"

I choked out a laugh. "Believe me, I'd rather style my hair with a chainsaw than help out Raul Barone. And if you don't spill, we'll both be sitting here until dawn."

He eyed me up, squinting into the shadows masking my face. I'd dragged the chair in front of the window, so the light from outside lit him and not me. Then he shrugged.

"What does it matter? My life's over just like Viv's. She dated that animal for months, right up until he tied her up, fixed her feet to a concrete block, and threw her in the river."

It was my turn to freeze, and for a second everything went black. When the world came into focus again, I'd slumped over the arm of the chair, and I struggled to get upright.

Leo shifted forwards onto his knees. "Are you okay?"

"Y-y-yes. I'm f-f-fine."

He crawled towards me, looking up at my face. "You don't sound fine. And you're shaking."

Was I? I held up a hand, and it quaked against the gloom. What do you know? Leo was right.

"I don't want to talk about it. I can't."

He came closer, reached up, and laid a hand on my forehead. "Lady, you don't look so good."

Beads of sweat dripped from my brow as I fell in

the water once more, the concrete block dragging me down, down, down. I held my breath, struggling against the current.

Or rather, against Leo. He picked me up like I weighed nothing and laid me on the bed. "Should I call an ambulance?"

"No!"

I'd only had a couple of full-blown panic attacks, both soon after the incident, and both times Emmy talked me through them. "Why is this h-h-happening again?"

Leo didn't answer, just gripped my hands as I kicked for the surface and dragged in air. Finally, finally, I could breathe again.

Oh, hell. As I came round, I saw the man I'd planned to intimidate watching me with fear in his eyes, not because he was scared of me, but because he was scared for me.

"What happened?"

I closed my eyes, screwing them up tight. But there was no getting out of it. Either I'd need to pull an outrageous lie out of the hat, or I'd have to go with the truth.

"That was me drowning," I whispered. "Almost. Raul tried to kill me too."

Leo stared at me for a half a minute, and I waited for him to say something. The usual, perfunctory, "I'm sorry," of a stranger pretending to be sympathetic.

But he didn't. He wrapped me up in his arms and held me close, stroking my hair. My brain told me I should fight free, that I needed to get the upper hand back in this situation and fucking well keep it, but the girl Vadim tossed off the bridge sagged against Leo.

His low voice soothed me. "I can't tell you it'll be okay because it won't, but I feel it too. Your pain."

And we sat there for two minutes, then five, ten, until I got myself back under control and untangled myself.

"I'm sorry."

"Don't be sorry. The only person who should be sorry is Raul Barone. And I intend to make him."

I looked up at Leo, realising too late I'd given him a clear view of my face. Fuck it. "And how do you plan to do that?"

He looked away, and I knew. "You have another knife, don't you?"

He stood up and stepped back. "You should leave."

"No way. Look, you can't kill Raul. Not that way. He has a bodyguard with him at all times, and he's sharp himself. Even if you did manage to pull it off, his family would hunt you down and gut you like a fish."

"You think I don't know that? I do. But I have nothing left. Nothing to lose."

If I'd had a heart, it would have ached for Leo. I couldn't let him go on a suicide mission.

"When did you lose your sister?" I asked, stalling for time.

"Eleven months, one week, and two days ago."

Before me. She was the girl before me. A fresh wave of revulsion came over me as I recalled seeing a pretty blonde in a couple of surveillance photos the Ice Cream Man had supplied. Was that Vivian? Had Raul killed her because I came on the scene? How could I tell Leo that?

"Almost a year."

"When she disappeared, I knew what he'd done. I

knew it right away. But they didn't find her body until six weeks ago. Kids found her. Kids, playing on the river bank. Their lives will never be the same again either."

If I hadn't been forced to leave my gun behind in Virginia, I'd have been tempted to march on board *Liquidity* and put a bullet between Raul's eyes. Vadim's too, the sadistic son of a bitch. But with Leo involved now, I needed to come up with a neater solution.

"Please just back off, for a week or two at least. I don't want Raul to get away with what he did either, but I'd rather live to see him rot."

"That's why you came as well, isn't it? Revenge."

"Yes." Another excuse wouldn't wash with Leo, and it was better than telling him I was working my way through a list of targets for cash.

"Then go home. Get on with your life and be happy. I'll take care of it."

"No, you won't." I refrained from adding, "Besides, I'll do a much better job."

"As long as he can't hurt another girl, that's all I care about."

"I'll help you. We'll come up with a plan, not some harebrained scheme that'll get us both killed."

A plan. Right now, my plan consisted of handcuffing Leo to something solid so he didn't screw everything up. Only I didn't bring any fucking handcuffs, either. Something else for my shopping list tomorrow, along with chocolate.

He raised an eyebrow. "So what was your idea? How were you going to get your revenge?"

"Uh, I hadn't entirely thought that one through." I mean, I had ideas, but they needed to be finessed. "I've only been here a few days, and I got distracted by you."

"We can't wait around. What if he sails off?"

"He won't. Trust me, he won't. He hates sailing, and he has business here."

"How can I trust you? So far all you've done is broken into my apartment and thrown a knife at me."

I held up a finger. "Past you, not at you."

And while I thought of it, I got up and wiggled it out of the wood, then pocketed it.

"You can't keep that."

"I don't trust you not to do something stupid."

He didn't say anything, and I knew if I didn't stop him he'd end up trying exactly that.

So I attempted to placate him. "Look, it's getting late. I'll see what Raul gets up to tonight so you can get some rest, and I'll watch him tomorrow. That way if Vadim has spotted you, it'll give him a day to cool off."

"You'll really do that?"

"Sure." After all, I'd been planning to do it anyway. "I'll come by tomorrow evening and we can toss some ideas around. How does that sound?"

He narrowed his eyes. "You swear you'll come back?"

"Cross my heart." Or even the ice-cold gap behind my rib cage.

He let out a long breath. "Okay."

Thank goodness. I tucked my zip-up sweater around me and took a step towards the door, then on impulse, I turned back and wrapped my arms around Leo.

"Thanks for being so sweet about all this. I'll see you tomorrow."

I looked up and met his eyes, which had widened in

surprise.

"Yeah, er, tomorrow."

I retreated, tucking my hands into my pockets. "Tomorrow."

As I jogged down the steps, I tightened my fingers around the cheap wood-handled blade I'd just removed from the small of Leo's back. He didn't even notice.

Amateur.

CHAPTER 11

WITHOUT HAVING TO worry about Leo butting in, I could give the plate of waffles my full attention the next morning. And *Liquidity*. Of course, I mustn't forget *Liquidity*. I could watch the boat too.

I forked in another mouthful of sugar and carbs as I thought over my chat with Leo last night. Why did I agree to work with him? In the harsh light of morning, logic told me I should have taken the sensible option and forced him to get the hell off the island. So, why hadn't I? I sighed because I knew the answer, and it wasn't just because Raul killed Leo's sister as well as trying to kill me. No, it was because I understood his pain more than I cared to admit. I'd lost a sibling too.

My bitch of a mom abandoned me in a hell-hole with my daddy, and I'd never, never forgive her for that, but worse was the fact that she'd stolen my brother from me. My eighteen-month-old brother, gone. I'd spent years looking for both of them, but they'd vanished from the face of the earth. For a brief moment, I'd wondered if my daddy murdered them both, but every week Mom used to hide the leftover grocery money in a tampon box in the bathroom, and when she disappeared, so did the cash.

Not only that, my daddy's fury in the days after they left was something he couldn't have faked. Believe me,

I still had a scar on my side to prove it. It was the only time he'd hit me, but the things he did after she went were far, far worse. Over the years, I'd had the other scars I accumulated removed by an excellent plastic surgeon, but that one...I kept it to remind me how far I'd come.

Mid-morning, Vadim lowered the gangplank and helped the secretary ashore, looking far from happy about it. His craggy face bore the same ugly glower he'd habitually worn when Raul ordered him to take me to the beauty salon. In fact, the only times I'd seen the man smile were when he was inflicting pain on somebody else. The night he tossed me into the water, he'd actually grinned.

So, from his expression I figured the secretary would live to suck another day, and I stuck with Raul. He meandered around the main deck on the phone for half an hour, then set his laptop up on the outside table at the rear of the salon. Working. And I needed that computer, or at least the contents. The question was, how did I get it?

Vadim returned two hours later with the bimbo, who'd had her hair done. It bounced around her face in those loose curls the shampoo ads always promised but never delivered. She pranced along the deck like a show pony, pressed herself up against Raul, and he soon put his laptop away.

I drummed my fingers on the table top, thinking. I'd never seen Raul take the laptop off the boat, which meant I needed to get on it. Easier said than done when it was habitually patrolled by a pitbull carelessly stuffed into a cheap suit. I'd need to pick my moment.

Vadim presented the biggest problem. Raul paid

him to be alert, so Raul himself could relax and not have to worry about little things like staying safe. That meant I'd need to deal with Vadim first. I'd just started plotting out various scenarios when something caught my attention on the dockside.

Or rather, someone.

Leo jogged past, followed by the gaze of every red-blooded woman in the vicinity. What the hell did he think he was doing?

My eyes cut to the stern of *Liquidity*. No, I wasn't the only one who'd noticed his antics. Vadim stood at the back railing, muscles flexed as he leaned on folded arms. Dammit.

Did Vadim realise the jogger was the same man who'd been sitting at the café all week? I'd be surprised if he didn't.

And just when I thought things couldn't get any worse, Leo came around for another circuit, then a third. Towards the end of the afternoon, as dusk rolled in like a fine veil, he strolled past, eating an ice cream while studiously pretending not to look at the boats. A twenty-something walked into a flower tub when Leo's tongue flicked out, and Vadim even sniggered at her plight. Me? I felt queasy, not just from the sight of the vanilla cone, but because I knew Vadim wouldn't let Leo's appearance slide.

Sure enough, when Leo turned off past the chandlery, heading in the direction of Seven Mile Beach, Vadim called out to his number two that he was leaving and jogged up the gangplank.

I slammed the lid closed on my laptop and followed.

The one good thing about the situation was that

Vadim focused all his attention on Leo, allowing me to move at the fast clip of a woman hurrying home after work as I trailed along behind both of them. I didn't want to make the same mistake as my nemesis, and I checked behind myself in windows as I walked, just in case Vadim had a friend I didn't know about.

Like a good little Girl Scout, I'd been prepared this morning and parked my moped near the bus stop. When Vadim flagged down a taxi to follow Leo, I hopped on and went along too.

Now, I had a decision to make. Did I keep behind or go on ahead? The sun dimmed with every passing minute, and Leo had bought groceries last night. Plus, he needed to go home because he was expecting me to visit. I'd put money on him not making a detour.

At the next set of traffic lights, I shot off in front of them.

Twenty minutes later, Leo turned into the street outside his apartment and walked right by the bush I was standing behind. Sure enough, his shadow followed fifteen seconds later.

I'd planned to watch Vadim until he left, to check he'd really gone before I went to ream Leo a new asshole, when the moody bastard jogged forward on silent, rubber-soled shoes, closing the distance between himself and his prey.

Shit. Vadim wasn't playing a waiting game tonight. He was going in right after Leo, and the stupid schmuck hadn't even noticed.

Visions of Leo tumbling from the upstairs window flashed through my mind, and I couldn't allow it to happen, no matter how much of a pain in my ass he might have become.

With no time to come up with a better plan, I sprinted forward, passing Vadim as Leo pushed open the outer door.

"Darling! You're home!" I affected Emmy's British accent as I threw myself at a startled Leo, plastering my lips to his as I shoved him through the door.

"What the—?"

I silenced him with my mouth, pinning him against the wall as I watched Vadim from the corner of my eye. He melted back into the darkness.

Keeping my head down, I took Leo's hand and led him into the stairwell.

"Have you lost your mind?" he half yelled.

"No, but you clearly have. Didn't you notice Satan's sidekick following you into the building?"

"Huh?"

"Vadim was right behind you."

"He was?"

I thunked my head back against the wall. "Why did you go to the marina today? You promised you wouldn't."

"I promised under duress."

"Bullshit. If I'd put you under duress, you'd have flown back to Atlanta last night."

"Okay, I went because I don't know you. How could I be sure you'd do what you said?"

I sat on a step, a little higher than him so our eyes were level. "This is wrong. We should be on the same side, and all we do is argue."

"Fine, so let's work together."

I didn't want to work with him. Apart from the odd job I'd done with Emmy, I always worked alone. But how else could I stop Leo from doing something stupid? I still hadn't bought handcuffs.

And right now, we had a bigger problem to deal with. "We can talk about that later, but first we have to get you out of here."

"What do you mean?"

"Vadim knows you're living here, so you can't stay."

He shook his head. "I don't have a choice. My rent's paid up until the end of the month."

"You'll just have to forfeit it and get a room somewhere else."

"I can't afford it." He sat next to me, elbows resting on his knees. "I spent almost everything I had on private investigators, and I'm down to my last few hundred bucks. I figured by the end of this month I'd be dead or in jail, so it didn't matter. I lost my job; I don't eat right, and I can't think straight." His voice trailed off to a whisper. "I'm nothing."

Fucking hell. Raul might have killed Vivian, but he broke her brother. Another victim of his endless cruelty. Leo said he felt my pain, but his rolled off him in waves, crashing into my senses and leading me to make an offer I'd never have made to anyone else.

"Stay with me tonight. We can sort something out in the morning. Neither of us is thinking straight this evening."

"Really?"

"It's the safest option." If Vadim showed up at my place, I'd kill him in self-defence and take pleasure in doing it.

"I don't even know your name."

"Call me Sasha."

The advantage of Leo having so little stuff was that it only took two minutes for him to pack. I retrieved the cash from the toilet tank while he shoved his clothes into a rucksack.

"How did you find that?" he asked, eyeing up the plastic bag.

"One of the first spots I looked yesterday. You need to think of a more original hiding place."

He sat on the edge of the bed and stared at the wall. "I'm terrible at this, aren't I?"

"Yes. But you'll get better."

"How? I'm not cut out for espionage."

"I'll teach you. Are you ready to go?"

"Who are you?"

No way was I about to tell him that. "I'm a nobody, just like you. But right now, I'm the nobody you'll need to trust if you want to take Raul down."

When he turned to face me, he met my eyes, and I caught a faint glimmer of hope where once there'd been none. "Okay. Let's do this. I promise I won't screw things up again."

"Better fucking hope not."

With the possibility of Vadim still lurking outside, we exited via the fire escape at the other end of the building. Thankfully, nobody followed as we hurried to my moped, parked a couple of streets away under the fronds of a leafy palm.

"This thing's underpowered for two people, but we'll have to manage."

"You want me to drive?" he offered.

I stared at him.

"I take it that's a no?"

"It's a no."

I started the engine, and Leo climbed on behind me, wrapping an arm around my waist as I pulled away. After having been on my own for so long, the human contact felt strange, like a jacket I'd admired in the store window for weeks but now I had it on, it didn't quite fit right. I wasn't sure whether I liked it or not.

When we reached my apartment building, Leo slung his bag over his shoulder and followed me up the stairs.

"Thanks for doing this. I mean, you didn't have to."

"Yes, I did. I can't stand the thought of Raul taking another life."

"Still, thank you."

I pushed the door open. "Have you eaten?"

"Not since breakfast."

"Then I guess that's our first job for the evening."

Five minutes later, we got into another argument. Were we ever going to have a normal conversation?

"Let's eat out," I suggested. "The kitchen's woefully inadequate."

"I don't have the money to eat out. I've turned into more of a noodles and salad kind of guy."

"I'll pay. Do you like Chinese?"

"You're not paying. That isn't fair."

"So it's more fair for me to live on noodles out of sympathy?"

"I didn't mean it that way. You're already letting me stay here, although I'm not sure where I'm meant to sleep."

He glanced round the room, taking in the only bed, still rumpled because I wasn't much of a housekeeper, and the tiny pink Energizer Bunny on the nightstand. Emmy had given it to me as a gift years ago, a reminder to keep going no matter what, and it went with me whenever I moved home. Leo picked it up and raised an eyebrow, which I ignored.

Okay, so I hadn't exactly thought things through either. There was no couch, just a rickety armchair, and I couldn't expect him to lie on the tiled floor.

"Share the bed. It doesn't matter." I hesitated, then shrugged. "I'm not attracted to men, anyway." Might as well get that out there to avoid any possible confusion farther down the line.

He raised an eyebrow. "You're a lesbian?"

"Not exactly. I just don't find most men do it for me. Or most women."

"Define most."

"Do we really need to have this conversation?"

"I'm intrigued now."

"Fine. For some inexplicable reason, I was attracted to Raul Barone. I think I had a breakdown or something. Satisfied?"

"Not by a long shot. And the women?"

"Woman. We messed around occasionally. It was only casual. Are you coming out for dinner?"

"I already said no to that. Why Barone? He sucked my sister in, but I can't understand what she saw in him."

"I'm not discussing Raul." And I was hardly going to dissect my miserable sex life with Leo. I'd only known him for two days, and I'd already had enough of him to last a lifetime. "I'm gonna get takeout. You can eat it or starve, and I don't care which."

Before he could get another word in, I walked out,

slamming the door behind me.

This. *This* was why I didn't want a man. They drove me crazy.

CHAPTER 12

I'D FOUND A Chinese restaurant I liked five minutes away, so it didn't take long for me to get back with a bagful of food. While I waited for the chef to do his thing, I'd wondered about the wisdom of leaving Leo alone in my apartment.

But we had to learn to trust each other. Like it or not, we needed to work together from now on.

When I got back and dumped the food on the table, Leo pretended to be disinterested, but his eyes lit up. Close up, with the lights on, I took the opportunity to study him better. In the photos I'd seen, he'd been built to perfection, but now his arms lacked definition and he'd lost weight. Too much weight. He hadn't had any fat on him in the first place, but now he looked positively skinny. Probably something to do with his "can't afford food" diet.

I shoved two-thirds of the cardboard containers in his direction. "Eat."

"I'll pay you back one day. I promise."

At least we'd moved on from "I'll be dead by the end of the month." I nearly told him not to worry about repayment, but I'd already wounded his pride quite enough over the past few days. "I'll hold you to that."

He ate fast, as if the food might disappear if he slowed down. I took my time, perusing the subtle differences in the room. The closet door, now slightly ajar. The bag of apples on the left of the desk when they'd been on the right.

"Did you find it?"

He looked up at me, pausing mid-chew. "Huh?"

"Cash, weapons, whatever you were looking for. Did you find it?"

"I didn't..." he started. "Okay, I looked. And no, I didn't find anything. You're better at hiding things than I am, I'll give you that."

Thank goodness he hadn't looked too closely at those apples.

"So, now what?" Leo asked after dinner.

He glanced towards the bed, but it was too early for sleep. Only half past eight. And too late to go to the marina. If Raul planned on heading out somewhere tonight, chances were he would've gone already.

And while I was out buying dinner earlier, I'd paid a quick visit to the pharmacy next door.

"I'm going to fix up your hair."

He brushed a hand back through the sandy ends and gave a nervous cough. "You're going to what?"

"You can't be blond anymore. Vadim's been looking at you all day. And the beard has to go." I picked up a pair of scissors. "First the hair."

"I'm not sure I want you near me with scissors."

"Would you rather it was Vadim?"

He sat back, and his white knuckles gripping the edge of the chair didn't go unnoticed. "Fine, get on with it."

I'd never win any contests, but I managed a passable cut—short at the sides, and slightly longer on top. "Now for the colour."

There was barely room for us both in the tiny bathroom, but we squashed inside, and Leo sat on the closed toilet as I donned a pair of rubber gloves and covered his hair in goo.

He'd stripped off his shirt before I started, in case of any accidents, and I'd been right about his loss of form. The abs that had once been pictured in a glorious eight-pack were barely visible. Leo looked like a blow-up doll someone had let half of the air out of.

"What happened to your muscles? I saw photos of you."

"The modelling?"

I nodded.

"After Viv disappeared, I put all my time into looking for her. Exercise fell into second place, and then I couldn't get modelling work anymore. I used to own a gym. Did you know that?"

"Yes."

"I lost that too. I mortgaged the place up to the roof to pay for a private investigator, and I couldn't afford the repayments." He pointed at himself. "So, here I am."

"We'll get the Raul problem sorted out, and then you can go home."

"I don't have a home either. Everything I own is in that bag out there. I couldn't even afford to give Viv a proper funeral."

A tear ran down his cheek, and I felt like a shit for starting this conversation. Passing him a wad of toilet paper seemed totally inadequate.

What would a normal person do in circumstances like this?

I channelled Mack—out of the Blackwood girls, she was the closest to sane—and patted Leo on the shoulder. "Things'll get better. You'll see."

"Forgive me if I don't believe you right now."

Leo sat in silence for the rest of the time it took for the dye to set, while I paced in the room outside. This situation was beyond awkward. Perhaps I should have taken Emmy up on her offer of help? Because now I was stuck with a goofy sidekick, and Raul was still floating in his fucking yacht on the fucking water.

The alarm on my watch pinged, and I rinsed the dye out of Leo's hair. I hadn't done a bad job if I said so myself.

His grimace suggested he didn't agree with me. "I'm not sure about the brown."

"Trust me; brunettes have more fun."

"Have you tried being blonde?"

"Several times." I dropped my voice to a whisper. "Most recently with Raul."

His hand on my arm made me jump.

"I'm so sorry that happened to you, Sasha. I wish I could have done something about him sooner."

"It's done now. Raul did his worst and I'm still here."

"But life will never be the same again."

"No, it won't."

I woke in the middle of the night with a prickling of the hairs on the back of my neck. Something was wrong.

My eyes popped open, and it took me a few seconds to understand the problem. I'd overheated. And the reason for that was Leo didn't understand the concept of his side of the bed versus my side of the bed. He'd crept across the invisible centre line and pressed up against me, leaving me hot and a little bit bothered. I'd only ever spent the night with Raul before, and he'd maintained a comfortable distance at all times. A cold distance. I understood that now.

Leo needed to learn some manners.

I lined up my hands and feet, then shoved. Only I misjudged slightly. This bed wasn't quite as wide as the one I'd been sleeping in at Emmy's place.

Leo's muffled voice floated up from the floor. "What the—?" Tousled brown hair appeared over the edge of the mattress. "Why did you do that?"

"You got too close. You were squashing me."

"It's not like I meant to. I was asleep, for goodness sakes."

"Well, you'd better... I don't know, train yourself or something. Stay on your side."

"Okay, okay. I'll try."

But he didn't manage it. By the time the sun rose, not only was he breathing noisily in my ear again, he'd slung an arm over my stomach. I peeled it away in disgust. Maybe we could find a camping store today and buy an air bed?

Hang on, did I just say "we?"

What was wrong with me?

"What's the plan today, boss?"

In the morning when we got up, I was pleased to see Leo had abandoned his ideas of doing this by himself.

"Raul never gets up early, so first I'm doing yoga, and then I'm going running. Are you coming? Or are you staying here?"

"I haven't gotten any exercise in a year."

"So, now's a good time to start, don't you think?"

"I guess. But I've never done yoga."

"We'll start with the basics. Fitness is important. If we need to run, or jump, or..." heaven help us, "swim, we have to know we can do it."

"But yoga?"

"Don't knock it until you've tried it."

Leo was already wearing shorts, and I spent the next hour teaching him sun salutations and the joys of the warrior asanas. To his credit, he picked things up quickly and didn't complain too much.

"Ready to run?"

He hesitated a second too long before answering. "Sure."

"Not too tired?"

"Nope."

Liar.

I'd bought him a pair of sunglasses yesterday, and a baseball cap, which helped to hide his looks. Although without the beard, even I barely recognised him as the man at the marina. He looked more like Leo in the old photos, at least from the neck up.

I took it easy on him as we jogged a couple of miles down Seven Mile Beach, then turned around and came back again.

"We're not going to the marina?"

I scowled at him. "Have you not learned anyt

"Sorry. I'm trying."

"Yeah, I'd noticed," I muttered under my breath.

"What was that?"

"Nothing. Look, let's shower and get some breakfast. I'm hungry already."

"So, this is where you've been hiding?" Leo mused, checking out Monty's.

"Hiding in plain sight, yes."

When I led Leo upstairs, Miranda did a double take and then grabbed my arm, holding me back as Leo sat down.

"You didn't say you had someone with you!"

And there was a fucking good reason for that. "Mostly he's busy in the daytime, which gives me plenty of time to write."

"If I had him hidden away, I'd never go outside."

I nearly offered him to her. She could keep him busy, and then I could get on with the Ice Cream Project. But that wouldn't be appropriate, would it? "It's difficult to drag myself away sometimes, but I have great willpower. Except when it comes to your waffles. They're delicious."

"Two portions?"

I glanced over at Leo, who was peering through the potted palm at *Liquidity*. "Yeah. Two portions."

Chapter 13

"SO, YOU SIT here all day?" Leo asked once he'd finished breakfast.

"Sometimes I follow if Raul or Vadim take a trip."

"Where do they go?"

"The bank. The occasional meeting. Raul's here on business, and Vadim visits the gym every afternoon."

Miranda came up with more coffee, and I caught her checking out Leo. Seemed he had an effect on everyone but me. And when Leo smiled at her, she poured his drink all over the saucer.

"Oh! I'm so sorry."

She grabbed a napkin from the next table and started blotting.

His smile didn't falter, and I couldn't help noticing his teeth. Was he genetically blessed, or had he just found a great dentist?

"These things happen. Here, let me help."

I rolled my eyes, and he smirked, just for a second. That confidence was something I hadn't seen from him before. A little of the old Leo, coming to the fore?

Once the mess was cleared and Leo had dug into a second portion of waffles, which Miranda brought over on the house, we got back to business.

"I need to get on that boat."

"Don't you mean we?"

"No, Leo, I mean I. Unless there's something you haven't told me, you don't know the first thing about breaking and entering, and besides, I need you to act as lookout."

"It seems like there's a lot you haven't told me as well."

"There is. And I intend to keep it that way. You're not getting on the boat, and that's non-negotiable. Believe me, I wish I didn't have to either."

"In case you get caught?"

"No." Oh hell, I might as well tell him. He'd find out sooner or later, anyway. "Because water freaks me out. Ever since that night, every time I go near it I panic. Even sitting here near the sea leaves me on edge. It took me days to be able to come in here."

I thought he might belittle me, and indeed I felt like a small child confessing to a fear of the dark. Who gets scared of water? But he didn't. Instead, he reached over the table and clasped one of my hands in both of his.

"Your hand's like ice. Have you been on a boat since the...accident?"

"Call it what it was—attempted murder. Sorry. I shouldn't have snapped." I sighed. Being near the wet stuff brought out the worst in me. "Twice. I've been on a boat twice, and I hated every second of it."

"But you did it. You're strong. Stronger than me. When the time comes for you to get on board *Liquidity*, I know you'll be able to."

Why did his words make me tearful? Was it because he had more faith in me than I had in myself? I resisted the urge to sniffle in front of him, hating the thought of painting an even weaker picture of myself, and extricated my hand.

"I need to use the bathroom."

Locked in a stall, I dabbed at my eyes with a tissue. Why had I broken down? I never used to get all emotional like this, even when I'd sunk into a depression. Those weeks, I simply stayed in bed. I thought back to a conversation I had with Emmy a few weeks ago, before Ripple and after I got back from a trip to Boston. She used to be the ice queen, but after a nasty incident with a drug lord and a rocket-propelled grenade, she said she started to feel things in a way she never had before. It brought home how delicate life could be. Had the same happened to me?

If so, I didn't like it.

When I got my sobs under control and stopped hiccupping, I went back out to Leo. He hadn't moved, other than to pick up his coffee and drink a quarter.

"You okay?"

"I'm fine."

"It's okay to grieve after what Raul did. He killed part of you that night, even if he didn't finish the job."

Tears threatened again. How did Leo find the words to express what I didn't understand myself?

"I can't carry on like this. I feel broken."

Leo scooted off his seat and slid onto the bench next to me. "Come here."

He opened his arms.

I hesitated. What comfort could I get from a man? They'd only ever hurt me in the past. But something drew me to him, and I nestled against his chest as he cocooned me.

"Is this the first time you've cried over him?"

"Y-y-yes."

"It's a good thing. Crying lets the pain out."

"D-d-did you cry? About Vivian?"

"For three days straight. And at the end of it, I got angry."

"I've been numb for months."

"Then cry. You'll feel better tomorrow; I promise."

And I did. In that quiet corner of a waterside restaurant, I wept for my former self. The confident girl who never let life get the better of her. And I wept for hope, the hope I'd had of finding a soulmate to spend my life with rather than going through it alone.

I sensed Miranda approaching, but Leo waved her away, leaving me to soak his shirt as agony poured out of me.

"I'm s-s-sorry," I told Leo.

He didn't sign up for this.

"Don't be."

Rather than shying away, he stroked my hair and tightened his arms around me.

I must have stayed there for half an hour, clinging to my lifeline in a stormy sea, but as the clouds above cleared and the sun peeped through, I saw a new dawn. And that crimson dawn was filled with fire and beauty. And anger.

I pried my face off Leo's chest and a slow smile spread across my lips. "I'm gonna kill that son of a bitch."

He grinned back. "Atta girl."

"Could you hold this table for us in the evening?" I asked Miranda with a shaky smile. I still felt embarrassed by my breakdown earlier.

"Dinner for two?"

I nodded. "We thought it would be nice to see the water at night."

"Are you okay? I mean, you looked real upset earlier."

"I just found out my grandma died."

She put a hand on my arm. "I'm so sorry."

"It was kind of expected. She's been fighting the Big C for two years now, but it still came as a shock, you know?"

"I lost my nana three years ago, and I promise the pain gets easier."

"I hope you're right."

With the booking sorted and my cover story in place, I led the way out of the restaurant, the need to plan battling with tiredness in my head.

"Where to now?" Leo asked.

"We have to get you a pair of glasses and a few other bits, and then I need a nap." I yawned. "I never normally get exhausted like this."

"Crying takes a lot out of you."

"Don't take the piss."

"I'm serious." He squeezed my shoulders. "Really."

He wasn't laughing, but I still wasn't sure I believed him when we reached the computer store. Oh, please let them have what I needed. I browsed the shelves until I found the holy grail—a one terabyte high-speed USB memory stick. I grabbed that, plus a couple of smaller sticks and a handful of assorted data storage cards, and then we moved on to the opticians.

"So, how do I explain that I want to buy glasses when I don't actually need them? Won't they think that's weird?" Leo asked.

I peered through the window, and luckily there was a woman running the place. "Leave it to me. Just keep out of the way for a minute."

I'd already embarrassed myself once today, so I might as well do it again. The job was far more important than my dignity—something I'd told myself on many occasions.

"He needs glasses," I explained to the assistant. "Two pairs."

She raised an eyebrow at Leo, who was browsing through the selection of frames. "Has he had a recent eye test?"

"Now here's the thing. His vision's fine. They're more for me." I dropped my voice to a whisper. "There's nothing sexier than a man in specs, and I want him to wear them when we...you know."

She glanced at Leo again, and this time her eyes dropped to his ass. So far, so good. "I'm sure I can help you out."

Half an hour later, Leo was the proud owner of a pair of chunky black frames, plus thinner silver ones. He clutched the bag as I led him towards our final stop, the pharmacy.

Once inside, I motioned to a spot by the door. "Wait here."

"I need razors."

"Okay, get them. Then come back here."

Of course, he didn't listen. Warm breath whispered across my neck as he reached forward and plucked a box from my hands. "Non-lubricated latex? Those aren't much fun. How about strawberry flavoured?"

I snatched the condoms back again. "They're not for sex, you idiot. I need them to keep the memory sticks dry. With all this water around, I'm not taking any chances."

He waggled his eyebrows. "There was I thinking you were gonna make me a happy man."

"I already told you, I don't like men."

"Good thing I only believe half the stuff that comes out of your mouth, isn't it?"

Somehow, we made it back to the apartment without me killing Leo, and I flopped back onto the bed.

"Wake me in a couple of hours, will you?"

He lay down beside me. "I'll set the alarm."

Great. "You'd better keep on your side this time."

He rubbed his hip. "I have a bruise."

"Good."

The world outside the window was dark when I woke up. Why was I so hot again? Uh oh. I unwrapped my arm from around Leo's chest and tried to extricate my leg from between his without waking him. I thought I'd managed it, but as I rolled back to my side of the bed, his hoarse whisper followed me.

"At least I didn't push you onto the floor for that."

What was I supposed to say to that? "Er, thanks."

He stretched his arms above his head and yawned. "It's late. You want to get dinner?"

Not really. I wanted to curl back up and go to sleep. Not with Leo, obviously. No way. Just me. "I guess we should go out."

The slim silver frames changed Leo's face in the way I hoped they would. Between that and the button-down shirt, he looked like a hot college professor. No.

No. A college professor. Not hot at all.

He held a hand out for me as we left the apartment, and I stared at it. "What's that for?"

"We're supposed to be acting like a couple, right? That's what the waitress at the restaurant thinks."

"We're not at the restaurant yet."

"Can you blame me for wanting to get into character a little early?"

I glared at him. "Can you stop with the whole sweet, flirty thing? It freaks me out."

"Sorry."

He wasn't sorry at all. He was laughing.

"Will you get on the damn bike?"

He climbed on behind and wrapped his arms around me. That didn't help either. This whole "working with a partner" thing was proving to be even more difficult than I thought.

Miranda went a tad overboard on the date night theme with candles on the table and complimentary glasses of champagne. When she wasn't looking, I leaned over and tipped mine in the palm pot.

"What did you do that for?"

"I don't drink when I'm working. If Raul and Vadim go into town tonight, I'm going on the boat, and being tipsy won't help matters."

I'd come prepared with memory sticks and condoms, but so far, they showed no signs of leaving. The lights in the salon blazed across the bay, and inside, I glimpsed Raul and the secretary seated at the table.

"Fair enough." Leo slid his glass over. "Can you get rid of mine as well?"

The palm certainly drank well that night. In fact, it probably had a more enjoyable evening than us. Between the water and a possible excursion onto *Liquidity*, I was on edge, and Leo's earlier flippant mood had turned melancholy.

"I miss her so much," he told me over dessert.

"Vivian?"

"Yeah. Growing up, it was just the two of us."

"What about your parents?"

"Mom liked the idea of kids, but after the first couple of years the novelty wore off and she ignored us. Dad worked all the time, and Mom went out with her friends, so I looked after Viv."

"That's tough. I've always thought people should have to take a test before they're allowed to have children."

"My parents would have failed for sure."

"Mine too." But I wasn't about to elaborate. "Do you speak to your parents much anymore?"

Emmy had thought not, last time I spoke to her, but it never hurt to check.

"They moved to Kansas years ago, and they didn't even bother to give us their new address. But it didn't matter. Viv grew up to be the sweetest girl, one I was proud to call my sister, despite the fact that their idea of parental responsibility was to leave a hundred dollars on the table after payday and leave me to feed us both."

"How did your sister get tangled up with Raul?"

"She always wanted to be an actress. She'd sneak into Mom's room and borrow her clothes to play dress-up, and at school, she lived and breathed the drama club. But do you know how difficult it is to get into that world when you don't know the right people? Almost impossible. She tried everything—local theatre, infomercials, movie extra work. Then she met Raul in a nightclub one night, and he told her he had contacts. Of course, the role didn't materialise, and the next thing I knew, she'd moved into his apartment."

"I bet he hated when she went out alone."

"I only saw her three times in the six months she was with him. Did he do the same to you?"

"He tried. I think that's one of the reasons he got sick of me—I insisted on keeping some of my independence."

"Viv wasn't strong enough to do that. He stole her whole identity and cut her off from everyone. She even changed her name. Viviana Moretti. She thought it sounded more exotic. Fuck, it hurts to talk about her."

This time, it was me who reached out for his hand. "He liked control."

"Yeah, but when she disappeared, he told me she'd decided to try her luck in Hollywood. By herself. As if she'd have done that."

I squeezed his hand in support. "Stop torturing yourself over it. I'll take care of him; I promise."

"That scares me as well. I don't care if something happens to me, but I worry about you."

"Worrying won't solve your problems, but it will steal your happiness." Emmy's husband told me that once, and I needed to live by it.

"I have precious little happiness to steal."

"Then we need to fix that too. Let's go home."

CHAPTER 14

MY PHONE RANG at six o'clock in the morning, and I unwound Leo's arm from around my waist, then slipped into the bathroom.

"Emmy?"

"Why are you whispering?"

I shoved the bathroom door closed with my foot. "I, uh... Leo's asleep."

I was surprised when her shriek didn't cause the building to disintegrate, let alone wake Leo. "You're sleeping with the hot dude?"

"No!"

"I thought you were staying in a one-bed apartment?"

"Okay, so we're sharing a bed, but we're not fucking. Clothes have remained firmly done up at all times."

"Hang on a sec... Bradley!" She dropped the phone and shouted for her assistant.

"You bellowed?"

"We need to organise a pool. Fia and Leo."

"That muscly guy Dan was drooling over?"

"Yup. Single day slots. I doubt this'll take long." There was a crackle as she picked up the phone again. "Sorry, you were saying?"

"Bitch, you can't start betting on my non-existent

sex life."

"Sure we can. Could you give me a hint as to how long this might take? I always lose, and fifty bucks is fifty bucks."

Like she cared when she was married to a billionaire. "It's not gonna happen. So far, I've had a panic attack in front of him and cried all over his shirt."

"And he's still there? Honey, it's gonna happen."

"It's not like that. Vadim found out where he was staying so Leo had to leave. I only offered him a place to sleep. And he makes a good cover story if I need to get dinner in the evening."

"You want me to courier over some nice underwear? You haven't gone all utilitarian again, have you?"

"Did you listen to a word I said?"

"Yeah, I just don't believe you."

I considered arguing, but with Emmy, I'd only have been wasting my breath. I opted for a subject change instead. "Can I borrow Mack again?"

"Sure. What for?"

I told her what I needed. A little out of the ordinary, perhaps, but a simple enough task for Mack.

"So, you have a plan?"

"Something's coming together in my head. But I need to get the computer files for the Ice Cream Man before I can have fun with the other stuff."

"You'll ace that. You know what?"

"What?"

"You sound better. Stronger. More like the old you."

"I don't feel like the old me. It's as if every emotion's amplified ten times over."

"Welcome to my new world. But it's not necessarily

a bad one, just different. Fuck your past, but don't let it fuck you."

"I've never been nervous before, not like this."

"Channel the energy into something more useful. Or better still, get Leo to take your mind off it."

"I'm going now."

"You should be coming."

Emmy couldn't be right, could she? As I slipped back into bed beside Leo, I dismissed the notion. Of course not.

"Are you ready for yoga?"

Leo groaned and rolled over. "I can barely move from yesterday's session. I ache in places I didn't know I had places."

"But it's a good ache, right?"

"It's the kind of ache I need a good physio and a handful of ibuprofen to take care of."

"I can help with the ibuprofen. Now, get out of bed. We have stuff to do."

Leo grumbled his way through ten rounds of sun salutations, then trailed behind me as I ran down the beach and back. When we got back to the apartment, he doubled up.

"I have a stitch."

He half-fell into the chair and leaned forward.

"You want water?"

"Thanks."

He didn't sit up, and I crouched in front of him with a glass. "You okay?"

"No." He groaned and straightened. "I hate what

I've turned into. A year ago, I wouldn't even have been breathing hard after that run. Now look at the state of me."

"You've only been running twice. It'll get better. And you can't give up. If you give up, Raul wins."

"Guess I'd better start eating better as well."

After my recent waffle-fest, I needed to join him. The top button of my jeans still strained when I did them up. "Fruit for breakfast?"

"Give me five minutes to take a shower."

Leo picked up a couple of paperbacks in a second-hand bookshop on the way to Monty's and took his place beside me while I typed away. I'd hit chapter seven in my pretend book—the arrival of a mysterious blond guy at the marina.

Now what? The story had started off as a thriller, but I was tempted to add some romance to it. You know, live vicariously through my characters? Give them what I never got.

Leo leaned closer. "You're writing about me?"

"No. This is fiction."

"A blond guy in a café? You expect me to believe that?"

"It's true."

"I told you before. I only believe half of what you say."

"I haven't got to the bit where my heroine pushes him off the top deck of a seafood restaurant yet."

"Your book's more exciting than mine."

And nothing was happening on *Liquidity*. Vadim

had jogged off to the gym, and Raul pored over his laptop while the secretary sunbathed topless. I watched as she slathered her breasts with sun cream and lay back down. Was my chest big enough? Did I need a bit of work?

Leo barely glanced up from his book. "Yours are nicer."

"What?"

"I know what you're thinking. And she's fake from the ground up. Not many men go for that."

I didn't know whether to slap him or thank him for the compliment. "You can't say things like that to me. And you're wrong. Raul obviously likes her."

He shrugged. "Someone needs to set you straight. And Raul's not a man. He's a monster, so I'd discount any opinion he has. But I'm curious. What did you see in him?"

My face flushed and I looked away. "I don't talk about that."

"So it was the sex?"

"Shut up." I slammed the lid of the computer down. "Nothing's happening. I'm going home until this evening."

A jazz quartet played softly in the corner of Monty's as we arrived for dinner, and most of the downstairs tables were already occupied. I still hadn't forgiven Leo for the overly personal comments earlier, and it hadn't helped when I'd migrated into his arms in bed again this afternoon.

"You can't keep buying me dinner," he said, as we

sat down.

"If it helps, think of this as a job. I'm in charge, and you work for me. Dinner goes on your expense account."

"That doesn't seem fair."

"And employees don't make inappropriate comments about their boss's breasts."

"They're nice. Why do you have such a problem with that?"

"Because it means you've been staring at them," I hissed.

"Sasha, you had them pressed against my chest while you snored this afternoon."

"I do not snore."

"It's more of a cute little snuffle-snort..."

"Shhh."

I waved a hand at him. I'd just caught sight of Raul and the secretary on the rear deck of *Liquidity*, and from the length of her skirt—belt—it looked like they were going out somewhere. Vadim materialised out of the darkness next to Raul, wearing a button-down shirt and tie. Around the boat, he stuck with a polo shirt. They were definitely going somewhere.

And that meant I was too.

A waiter stopped by the table, pad and pen in hand. "Are you ready to order?"

I gave my head a shake, and Leo took over before I could speak.

"Actually, my girlfriend's feeling a little ill. I think I'm going to take her home. Right, sweetheart?"

"Sorry. I was fine when we left, but I've gotten all queasy."

The waiter stepped back as if he might catch

something. "These things happen. I hope you feel better tomorrow."

I managed a wan smile. "So do I."

Leo tucked an arm around my waist and helped me down the stairs. "Now what?"

"Alley next to the chandlery. Go down it."

I swayed slightly as we walked, adding to the illusion of a merry couple out for a bit of fun, and we made it to the alley before Raul got off the boat. The secretary had disappeared into the main cabin. She'd forgotten something. Her brain?

"We wait here until they go, then head for the boat next to *Liquidity*. It's been deserted for three days, and my source says the owner's flown to Florida for the week. In the meantime, if anyone stops by here, kiss me."

"Kiss you?"

"We're supposed to be a drunk couple, remember? The only reason for us to stop in an alley is for a quick fumble."

"Oh, right."

He slid an arm around me, and I confess to feeling slightly disappointed when no unwanted visitors showed up. Then I told myself not to be so stupid. After all, I didn't want any more emotional entanglements. This job had cost me enough already.

Not to mention the fact I didn't voluntarily do men. And certainly not Leo.

"Ready?" I whispered.

Raul, Vadim, and the secretary had climbed into a cab ten minutes ago, so I gave them five more in case they forgot anything else and decided to return before we made a move.

"Is it normal to be nervous?" Leo asked.

In the past, never. But now? "I sure as hell am. Keep your head down as you go. There's a security camera over the café, and we'll be on film for a few seconds. There's also a pair of roving security guards, but they went past five minutes ago, and they're not due back for another fifteen."

Leo got into character as he escorted me across the quayside, managing to wrap me up in both his arms as well as pausing to press his lips to my cheek halfway. Goosebumps popped out all over me, strictly from the cool night air, you understand.

On board *Liquidity*, lights shone from the windows of the crew quarters as we passed. By my reckoning, the captain, the deckhand, and Vadim's lackey were still on board, but they wouldn't be expecting company. I'd get past them, no problem.

Only one group of people were in sight as we approached the boat beside *Liquidity*, and they were all facing in the opposite direction as Leo and I leapt the five-foot gap between the dock and the swim platform. The tides were such that the two were almost level, and I hoped we'd be finished before the sea level dropped much lower. Otherwise getting back to shore would be tricky without a gangplank.

As soon as we got on board, I led Leo around to the bow of the boat and found him a nice spot in the shadows.

"If you see any movement on board *Liquidity*, or anyone heading in her direction from the quayside, call me, okay?"

I'd set both of our phones to vibrate earlier and made sure they were fully charged.

"Got it."

I checked my pockets. Yep, I had the memory sticks, condoms, my phone, and the cash I hadn't needed for dinner, all securely zipped in. I slipped on a thin pair of leather gloves and handed a second pair to Leo, just in case. No more stalling.

"Wish me luck."

He reached out and squeezed my hand. "Good luck, Sasha."

Without further ado, I turned and vaulted the port rail, then leapt the three-foot gap onto *Liquidity*.

The boat was pretty much as I remembered, except when I picked the door into the salon, I saw that Raul had replaced the carpet in there with something even more hideous. The pattern looked like someone had steamrollered Big Bird. Now, where was that damned laptop?

I couldn't see it lying around the salon, and I'd never seen Raul venture to the bridge, so I headed below. The sound of a television floated through the door that led to the crew quarters, tucked away in front of the engine room, and I crept past into the largest stateroom. Raul's bedroom, and one I'd once shared with him. When I thought of what we'd done on that bed, I wanted to be sick.

But then I spotted Raul's laptop, sitting open on his desk next to the dregs of a glass of whisky. He always had been careless about locking it in the safe, the arrogant bastard, and I'd been counting on that.

The thing seemed to take forever to turn on, but the second the cursor in the password box blinked at me, I jammed the big memory stick into the nearest USB port and said a silent prayer that the program Mack had sent me would do what she promised.

"It's simple," she'd told me two days ago. "Just insert the stick in the slot and wait. It'll suck in the entire hard drive, encryption and all. Then you send it to us, and we pull the data out at our leisure."

She'd put the emphasis on simple, but she should have put it on wait. Thirty-one minutes remaining. What the fuck did Raul keep on this thing?

As I listened at the door for any movement, I cursed myself for not having done this while I was living with Raul. Every day I'd put it off, telling myself tomorrow there'd be something more worthwhile to steal, when in reality, all I'd wanted was one more orgasm. And now, as my nerves stretched to their breaking point, I was paying the price.

Eleven minutes to go, and the sound of a door opening sent me scuttling into the bathroom, waiting to incapacitate anyone who might walk in. But then a distant toilet flushed and all went quiet again.

Until, with three minutes to go, footsteps sounded in the narrow corridor outside, soft but hurried. A door opened, then another. Two fucking minutes left. I took my position behind the bathroom door again.

Over two years had passed since I'd killed anybody with my bare hands, and despite a few sessions with Emmy's sadistic personal trainer when I visited Virginia, I had a sudden panic that I might fuck things up. Especially if it was Vadim. That man was built like a nuclear bunker.

Sure, I could use a knife, but that would create its own problems. I ran my fingers over the Emerson CQC-7 folder clipped to my waistband, a gift from Emmy. Tempting but too messy.

The door flew open, and I gave the intruder two steps to get into the room.

Then I stopped mid-lunge, my hands outstretched.

"Leo? What the fuck are you doing here?" I spoke in a harsh whisper.

He turned, wide-eyed in panic. "They're here. You need to get out!"

"Who? Raul and Vadim?"

"Raul and the woman are up on deck having an argument. Something about a text message and a hooker."

"Dammit." I leapt back to the computer. "One minute."

"Now. We have to go now." Fear made his voice shake.

"Why didn't you call me?"

"I did, six times. It went to voicemail."

I quickly checked my phone. No signal. The boat hull must have been blocking it. Shit.

Then the bar on the laptop screen turned green, and I tore the memory stick out of the machine and held the power button down until it switched off.

"Right we're out of here."

Voices sounded nearby as the crew joined in the party. Not good. Leo's eyes cut towards the closed door, widening in fear. No, we wouldn't be slipping out that way, not with company coming. We needed a new plan.

Well, this was why they paid me the big bucks.

That kick of adrenalin I secretly loved rushed through my veins as my mind cycled through the options. Fight? Hide? Or something more devious...

Okay, time for plan B.

CHAPTER 15

"HOW? HOW THE hell do we get out of here?" Leo asked, panic in his voice.

"Emergency escape hatch." I pointed at the ceiling. "Lift me up."

I wanted to avoid screaming "intruder" by using the ladder if possible, and Leo lifted me like I weighed nothing. Guess he still had some of that strength left. I cracked the hatch open and peered through the gap—all was still, so I opened it fully and hauled myself out.

"Come on."

I reached down for Leo, but he took a running jump and pulled himself through. Nice.

I flipped the hatch shut, tugged Leo into a crouch behind a sun lounger, and took stock of the situation. Raised voices came from the stern, first Raul's, then the high-pitched screech of a woman.

Maybe we could wait it out?

Then both of them were eclipsed by Vadim's booming shout, his Russian accent coming out as he got agitated. "Why is this door unlocked?"

Or maybe not.

I stuffed the memory stick in a condom and knotted the end, knowing in my heart what was coming next and dreading it. Footsteps sounded on the side gangways, flashlight beams sweeping from side to side as Vadim organised the crew to search.

Leo looked at me. "We're getting wet?"

I nodded, teeth clenched.

"Will you be okay?"

"I'll have to be, won't I? Ready?"

With no more time left, I ran for the bow and dived over the railing, landing in the water with barely a splash. Leo followed me in, and I grabbed his hand as I stroked for the bow anchor chain.

Lights played over the water as Vadim looked for us, and I knew we wouldn't be able to return to the boat next door. We'd have to swim farther.

Now, I'd been taught to free dive by one of the best —Emmy's husband, in fact. I'd known him to swim over a hundred yards underwater on one breath, and static, he could hold his breath for almost ten minutes. I wasn't on his level, but I could manage fifty yards without a problem. The question was, could Leo?

Right at that moment, I didn't even know whether he could swim.

I motioned towards the boat he'd been on, signalling that we needed to swim underneath. He nodded and we set off, but as we went to come up in the gap on the other side, the water above us lit up. Fuck. I dragged Leo down again, but I saw from the panicked look in his eyes he wouldn't last the swim to the next boat.

What could I do? Nothing but grab his face in my hands and force half of my air between his lips, then carry on swimming. If Vadim's crew had got as far as the next boat, we'd be finished.

We came up gasping, both of us, and I gripped Leo's hand. "We need to keep going, one boat at a time, to the end of the marina. Understand?"

He nodded, took a couple of deep breaths and dove under again, leaving me to follow. Three boats, four, six, ten, fourteen... It seemed like forever before we reached the end of the row, and from the look of *Liquidity*, lit up like a beacon against the inky sky, Vadim was still searching for his intruder.

"You're good at this," I whispered to Leo, my teeth already chattering, not from the cold but from fear. I needed to get out of the water, but I couldn't, not yet.

"I was on the swim team in high school, but I never had to hold my breath like that. How did you learn?"

"I had a good teacher, but what improved things was being shot at by drug traffickers off the coast of Mexico. Are you ready to go again? We need to head down the shore until we find a good place to get out and lie low."

"I'll follow you."

Stars twinkled overhead as we leapfrogged along the coastline, one mansion at a time. When we'd swum half a mile, I started looking for a suitable exit. There— that house looked good. Dark and deserted, with a hotchpotch of landscaping near the water's edge. I motioned Leo ashore and hunkered down in front of a summerhouse, hidden from view by a monstrosity of a brick grill and a collection of scattered plant pots.

In the distance, the engine of a jet ski roared to life, and I knew Vadim was out searching. He didn't give up easily.

"Should we go?" Leo pointed towards the front of the house.

"Not yet. We're both soaked through, and if anyone sees us, that'll arouse suspicion. Vadim's on his own searching from the water—Raul won't get his hands dirty, and I bet the others will be checking from the shore. Better we stay here until we stop dripping."

I tilted my head to the side and squeezed the water out of my hair. With all the salt, it would dry stiff and wild. Something else I didn't miss about the sea. I glanced back out to the inky blackness and shivered at the thought of what we'd just been through.

"Cold?"

"A little." Despite the warm temperatures, I'd soon get chilled from the evaporating water. "But mostly freaked out about the swimming. How are you not?"

"Because we survived." He parted his legs and patted the space between them. "Come here. We can keep each other warm."

I crawled over, and he wrapped his arms and legs around me, resting his chin on my shoulder. That shouldn't have helped, seeing as Leo irritated the shit out of me, but weirdly I felt more relaxed. Safer. A crazy thought when I had the knife, not him.

As his body heat spread through me, I wrapped my arms around his and leaned back against his chest. Maybe I'd been a bit harsh with my original deflated-doll comment, because tonight, his chest didn't feel bad at all. Certainly more solid that Raul's, that was for sure.

"Did you get what you needed?" Leo asked.

"The files? Yeah."

Half the job was done. Well, it would be once I sent the files to Emmy. She'd hold onto them until completion. Although I'd worked for the Ice Cream Man for years, I didn't trust the fat fucker as far as I could throw him. If I handed over Raul's secrets right away, he'd start tinkering, and most likely his efforts would send Raul running back to Atlanta. And that wouldn't do. I needed him here for phase two.

Leo ran his fingers through my hair. "It's drying."

I reached back and did the same to him. "It's dry."

He laughed. "That's because you cut most of it off. And speaking of cutting things off, what do you have planned for Raul? Your face... It has that thinking look."

"What thinking look? You can't even see my face."

"I can see your mouth. It twitches, right here."

He pressed a finger to the corner.

Dammit. I never used to give myself away like that. The old me had mastered the blank mask. *The old me.* Would I ever find her again?

"Sasha, you're shaking. What's wrong?"

"I'm cold."

"That's not it. You're thinking about him again, aren't you?"

I closed my eyes. "I can't help it."

"Try. He's not worth it."

"I know. But..."

"But what?"

"No other man made me feel like he did. And what if I go the rest of my life without feeling that way again?"

"Do I need to remind you he tried to kill you?"

"I know!" I gripped my hair in frustration. "My head knows that, okay?" It was just my body that had a hard time getting the message.

"So, how did he make you feel?"

"It doesn't matter."

"Yes, it does, because you're tense as hell, and he's

taking up space in your head that he has no right to."

I let out a low groan. I couldn't believe I was having this conversation with Leo, of all people. "Sexy. He made me feel sexy, okay?"

Leo chuckled softly behind me. "That's it?"

"Shut up! I wish I'd never told you. No other man has even gotten close to making me come. And it doesn't work when I try it myself either." Fuck. My brain-to-mouth filter needed serious work.

But he kept laughing. "Then you've been with the wrong men. Either they didn't bother to try, or they didn't know what they were doing. Lazy bastards."

"But what if it's me?"

"It's not you."

"You don't know that."

"I know you're sexy." He pulled off his gloves and nuzzled my ear. "Since we have nothing better to do than sit around at the moment, let's try a little experiment."

A flash of heat shot through me as his teeth nipped my earlobe, and I twisted to look at him. "What kind of experiment?"

"Face the front."

"What are you doing?"

"Trust me. You asked me to trust you, and I did. Now I'm asking you to do the same."

"Why?"

"Stop asking questions," he whispered. "Just do it."

I must have lost my mind because I did as he wanted. This was wrong, all wrong, but I couldn't help myself.

Leo's raised the hem of my shirt, and I stiffened. Warm fingers paused below my bra, then continued upwards until he palmed my breast. All I felt was a vague sense of unease as old memories stirred inside me, and I shoved those thoughts deep into a recess in the back of my mind, taking comfort in the numbness that took their place.

But Leo didn't stop. He slid his hand inside my bra cup and a rough digit brushed over my nipple. Honestly, what was the point in this?

A puff of breath passed over my cheek as he rolled my nipple between his thumb and finger. Okay, that was sort of nice but far short of spectacular.

"How does that feel?"

I shrugged. "All right. Nothing special. I told you, I'm broken."

I mean, Emmy did this thing with her tongue and it felt good, but apart from that, my breasts had never given me any... "Fuck!"

Leo pinched my peak, hard, and a bolt of...something shot through me. Pain? Pleasure? It was hard to tell.

Another chuckle in my ear. "Ah, you felt that." His other hand slipped under the waistband of my shorts. "Right here, didn't you?"

"Uh..."

"No need to answer. I know."

The top button on my shorts popped open, and then he slid the zipper down. I went rigid as a finger slipped under the edge of my panties, and I wasn't the only thing to stiffen if the stirrings I felt in the small of my back were to be believed.

Leo's finger grazed...well, on his more romantic days, Raul had called it a jewel, but I always thought of it as the uncut version. And not a lot happened. I leaned back and sighed. Maybe he'd give up soon, and we could go home?

He slid his hand out and held a finger to my lips. "Suck."

"What? Yuck, no."

He pressed harder, and I yielded, allowing his digit into my mouth. I could taste myself on him, and it made me cringe. Then he moved his hand back, and this time his lubricated finger slid over my jewel as he pressed harder. Ohhh. He did that thing to my nipple again, and this time I couldn't stop my back from arching. Before I straightened, he bit my earlobe, hard this time, and another fizz of electricity jolted through me.

"Ah, you like it a little rough."

Did I? At that moment, I didn't know what I liked. Everything felt strange.

Leo shoved his hand farther between my legs, and I clamped my thighs around his arm as he stroked again.

"You dirty little minx. You're getting wet."

We were supposed to be getting dry. "Leo, stop."

He stilled. "Do you really want me to?"

Did I? I rubbed against his hand, and my stomach clenched. "I don't know what I want."

"I do."

His finger moved again, pressing into me, and I gasped. Leo wasn't supposed to make me feel like this. So dirty, and...hot. I mean, this was Leo.

Then one long finger pushed inside me, stroking, as the other hand tweaked and grabbed. Fingernails raked along the inside of my thigh, leaving a stinging trail as they went. Then he added another finger and I struggled in his arms, not to get away, but to get closer to whatever he was doing. Teeth attacked my neck, and I didn't know which way to move. What was this man? A bloody vampire?

His thumb joined in, and I grimaced at the squelching sound. Was that coming from me? Fuck. Then I gave up trying to think and surrendered to him.

My whole body quivered, and he stuffed my T-shirt in my mouth. I tried to speak, but all that came out was a silent scream as I fell apart beneath his hands.

Holy fuck!

Before I came back to earth, Leo had rearranged my underwear, pulled my T-shirt down, and done my shorts up.

"There. Did I make my point? Raul's nothing special."

CHAPTER 16

THE LAST SHIVERS of the best orgasm I'd ever had quaked through me as I stared into the darkness. Vadim could have put a gun to my head right now, and I'd have been powerless to stop him. Fuck.

What the hell just happened? My mind struggled to process it: the pain, the pleasure, the way the two came together and made me fly. Was Leo right? Had some connection in my brain got frazzled so the sting of a man's fingers turned me on? All my adult life I'd worked on inflicting pain, not relishing it, and the whole concept left me confused as hell.

Another thought slammed into me—was that why Raul had succeeded where others had failed? He'd never hurt me, well, at least until he had me thrown off a bridge, but in the bedroom, he'd been pushy. Selfish. He'd taken what he wanted, and like an idiot, I'd been thankful for the leftovers.

The words "too stupid to live" flitted through my head as a dog barked in the distance.

Leo ruffled my hair. "Almost dry. Can we go now?"

"Uh…" In my head, I knew what words were, but I was buggered if I could string them together into a sentence.

The git only smiled. Smug. And I grudgingly had to admit that he had every right to be.

He tipped me to the side, stood up, and held out a hand. "Come on."

Come on what? His fingers again? *Oh, shit, Fia. Stop thinking like that. Concentrate on the job.* I ignored Leo and used the handle on the summerhouse door to pull myself to my feet.

"Okay, home."

I could do this. One foot in front of the other. Simple.

Leo pulled me tight against his side, and my hand slammed into his chest. "What are you doing?"

"The cover story? The whole drunk couple thing?"

"Oh, yeah. Right."

We skirted around the edge of the property, mindful of any security lights, but nothing blinked on. A few minutes later, Leo gave me a boost over the front wall, then climbed it himself.

"Okay?"

"Mmm."

No. Not at all. My world had just shifted on its axis. Could Leo be right and the only thing wrong with me was that I had terrible taste in men? Had I wasted an entire decade of...what he just gave me?

"Head down."

I looked away as a car sped past. Raul? I'd missed its approach completely. My head was filled with mush —random sensations of drowning and being brought to life. I gave it a shake to try and clear it. I needed to get back in the game.

By forcing myself to concentrate, I visualised the maps of the area I'd studied for so long and pulled Leo down a side street. "Shortcut."

Twenty minutes later, I was relieved to find the

moped right where we'd left it, parked outside someone's house so as not to stand out. I hopped on in front and Leo took his place behind.

As I rode back, all I could think of was his arms around me, his chest pressed into my back. I was in trouble.

Leo yawned the second we walked through the door. "I need to sleep."

I didn't get a chance to reply before he dropped onto the bed and closed his eyes. His breathing rate slowed as he drifted off. While he slumbered in peace, I sat on the wooden chair, rueing the fact I had no alcohol in the apartment, because I really, really needed a drink right then.

But I couldn't stay there forever. Like it or not, I needed sleep too and the only place I'd get that was next to Leo. When my eyelids began to close of their own accord, I lay down beside him and let them.

I woke to the smell of coffee and rolled over to find myself alone in bed. The bathroom door was closed, but two steaming mugs sat on the counter. I stumbled towards them, patting down my crazy hair as I went.

Leo came out as I took my first sip. "Sleep well?"

"I think so. I can't remember."

Did I blush when I said that? Because I could remember. I'd dreamed of him, feeling him behind me again with his fingers doing all those things they shouldn't.

"Good. So, what are today's plans, boss?"

"I haven't thought about it." But we needed to talk.

"About yesterday…"

"Which bit? The bit where you stole Raul's data? Or conquered your fear of water? Or afterwards?"

"Afterwards." And I hadn't conquered my fear of water. If anything, it was worse. I didn't even want to get in the shower this morning. "What happened between us?"

"A brief moment of distraction. I'm not going to start mauling you as we sleep, if that's what you're worried about."

"I'm not worried." In fact, now he'd mentioned it, I was more curious than concerned.

"Good. Because it didn't mean anything." He squeezed my shoulders. "Between you and me, you're not my type. I just didn't want you going through life thinking Raul was something to aspire to."

Not his type? That stung far more than it should. "Thank goodness. I didn't want things to change between us because of one insane moment."

He grinned. "I'll keep my hands off. No problem. So, today's schedule?"

Okay, mind back on the job. "We need to stay away from the marina. I don't want to spook anyone. And I need to start uploading the data to one of my contacts because that's gonna take ages."

"You want me to go out and get something for breakfast while you start that?"

"Please. I'm starving."

He fished in his pockets and dropped his voice. "Any chance I could borrow some cash?"

I knew how much it hurt him to ask that. "In the tampon box in the bathroom."

"No wonder I didn't find it."

The mobile internet connection was surprisingly good in my tiny abode, but even so, the data for Mack would still take over twenty-four hours to upload. I emailed to warn her it was coming, then pushed the "send" button.

And that left me the rest of the day to plot and plan and scheme. After Leo's revelation last night, the last barrier in my mind to killing Raul had been removed. But how could I do it with a clean getaway?

By making it look like an accident, or at the very least muddying the waters, that was how.

I'd use my old favourite.

Poison.

Some of my colleagues liked to get up close and personal, to see their victims die with their own eyes. But me? Yes, watching could be satisfying, but I took the greatest pleasure in knowing a man died by my hand when I wasn't even in the room.

As a small child, before I discovered guns and boys, I'd used fairy tales as my escape, although I found the happily-ever-afters a little depressing. After all, that didn't happen in real life, did it? In my head, I twisted them, adding a touch of realism. What would have happened if Cinderella hadn't lost her shoe? If the woodcutter hadn't happened across Red Riding Hood? If Snow White had swallowed the apple?

As I got older, I found out some of the answers. No prince came to save me after my first party. A classmate got mauled by a wolf on a hunting trip. And when I fed my daddy a poisoned apple, he died.

Ever since he breathed his last, I'd been fascinated

with how such tiny amounts of a substance could affect the human body. Back then, I'd used digitalin, a somewhat impure version I'd extracted from the foxglove plants myself. But over the years, I'd refined my methods and the apple trick only got better.

It was why they called me Snow.

With Leo still out, I lay back on the bed, thinking things through. I had a few ideas, but getting hold of the right poison would be key. Not that I didn't know where to find it. I did. I just didn't want to fetch it.

My spare phone rang, breaking me out of my thoughts. The other one had drowned last night, along with Leo's.

"Congrats on last night. Where are you?" Emmy asked.

"In my apartment. Why?"

"You spooked Raul. He's on the move."

"Shit. Where?"

"Not sure yet, but *Liquidity* just cast off. Mack's watching via satellite."

A key rattled in the lock as Leo came back with two carrier bags. He held up a plastic package of waffles and grinned, but I'd lost my appetite.

"Can you track her? I'll start packing."

"Already am."

I tossed the phone down on the bed and sighed. Why did Raul have to make things so fucking difficult?

Leo perched on the chair and raised an eyebrow. "Packing?"

"Raul's leaving, which means I am too."

He looked hurt. "You mean we are."

I shuffled up the bed so I could look at him. He'd been through hell, first with his sister, then with his own life, and again last night with me. And still he smiled. I didn't want to be the one to make him suffer more.

"I can do the last part by myself."

"We started this together, and we'll finish it together."

"Leo, no," I whispered. "Go home. It may not seem like it at the moment, but you have everything to live for, and I don't want to drag you down."

"I found him once, and I'll find him again. I'm still coming."

"We're talking about killing a man." I let out a thin stream of breath. "And I've done it before. I promise I won't fuck things up again. It'll get done."

"I figured you had." He stared at the wall beyond my head. "And I'm not going to ask for the details. But even if I only help by making you dinner each night, I'm not letting you go through this alone."

"Dinner?"

He nodded at the tiny kitchenette. "Maybe the next place we stay will have more than a microwave?"

I was stuck with him, wasn't I? And damned if I couldn't get too upset about that. I managed a small smile.

"I'll see what I can do."

CHAPTER 17

"WHO WERE YOU talking to on the phone?" Leo asked.

I'd unwrapped one of the waffles and taken a mouthful, but it was dry and bland. Not a patch on Monty's.

"An acquaintance."

"Someone who's helping with this...thing?"

"Yes."

Leo looked around the room, his gaze alighting on the window. "Is he here on the island?"

"She. And no, she's not."

"Then how...? No, I won't ask."

I chucked the rest of the waffle in the trash and stuffed my belongings in my bag. Leo watched from the bed as I unscrewed the broken air conditioning vent from the wall and retrieved more cash and my weapons.

"Here." I threw his knife back to him. "Promise you won't do anything stupid with that."

He held up his hands. "I'm leaving things to the expert from now on."

Then I paced. The repetitive motion soothed me as I walked up and down the tiny room, but I suspect it irritated Leo. In the end, he got up and went for a proper walk.

I'd been prepared for a long wait, but Emmy called back sooner than expected.

"Raul hasn't gone far."

"He's still on the island?"

"Moved to a private mooring farther along the coast. Guess he didn't like the traffic through the marina."

"Can you get me pictures?"

"Check your email."

A few seconds later, they pinged into my inbox. Well, I could kiss a decent breakfast goodbye. *Liquidity* was anchored up outside a mansion, surrounded by other mansions. And even more mansions after that. Not a restaurant, café, or store in sight. No more brunch and no more skulking in alleys for me.

Private homes, especially the size of those, meant private security, floodlights, alarms, and dogs.

"Fuck it."

"He's sublet the berth through the yacht club and paid two months up front." A pause. "How much do you love me?"

I heard the smile in her voice and groaned. "What have you done?"

She'd used the same tone when she arranged a surprise parachute jump for my birthday. Tandem. And she paid extra for the instructor to be naked.

"See the house with the dolphin pool? Two doors up?"

"Yeah, I see it."

The dolphin was done out in blue mosaic, made all the more tacky by the dolphin fountain and dolphin-shaped flower beds.

"A hot model's just rented the place for the next

quarter. He wants a bit of alone-time with his girlfriend."

"So?"

"That's you, you idiot."

"You rented me a house?"

"You and Leo. You can thank me properly when you get back to Virginia."

"No threesomes."

"Aw, you break my heart. I'll settle for you getting some hot-model action."

"Emmy…"

"I'm only thinking of you."

I clenched my thighs at the memory of Leo's particular brand of action, then quickly shook it out of my head. *Concentrate, Fia.*

"I'll bring candy." The expensive kind. "If we've got a permanent base here, I can install cameras too. Any chance…?"

"Every chance. I'll get Mack to sort out what you need and send it by express courier. You want us to set up a remote system so we can help with the surveillance from here?"

The chance to offload the most boring part onto somebody else? "You sure know how to make a girl happy."

Emmy chuckled. "You of all people should know that."

I hung up and leaned back against the counter. Emmy had come through and rented the perfect place for us to spy on Raul. And knowing her, she'd funnelled it through so many shell companies the owner wouldn't have known whether the true occupant was the pope or Lady Gaga.

Leo came back ten minutes later, still looking worried. "Any news?"

"We're getting a better kitchen."

Between the two of us, we had too much stuff to carry on the moped, so we picked up the key from the rental agent and rode over with my bag first only to find the house came with an SUV for guest use. Thanks, Emmy.

After a brief argument about who got to drive, I climbed behind the wheel, and we drove back for Leo's bag.

"The rental lady was nice, wasn't she?" Leo said. "It was kind of her to give us that bottle of champagne."

"She checked out your package, then your ass when you turned around." And I'd nearly poked her fucking eyes out.

Leo waggled his glasses at me. "Must be these. Maybe she has a fantasy."

One night over dinner, I'd told him what I said to the optician, and now he reminded me at every possible opportunity.

"No, I don't think that was it."

He grinned. "Then what?"

"Maybe you had dirt on your pants."

"And maybe you have dirt in your mind."

This new, happier Leo was driving me insane. Thank goodness we'd be in separate beds tonight. No more waking up tangled in his arms. And legs. That was a good thing, right?

When we got into the new house, I ignored the master suite at the front and dumped my bags in the second smallest of the bedrooms at the back. *Liquidity* bobbed in the gentle swell beyond next-door's waterside dining area. I leaned my hands on the windowsill, my face an inch from the glass.

"Nice view." Leo's voice came from the doorway.

"With a pair of binoculars, it'll be as good as Monty's."

"Oh, you can see the boat from here?"

I turned around and saw where his gaze was directed. "And you accuse me of having a dirty mind?"

He chuckled. "I'm going to make dinner. Any requests?"

"No, I'll eat anything."

"I'll remember that."

I watched the boat for half of the evening, at which point Raul decided to take advantage of *Liquidity*'s new-found seclusion and fuck the secretary on the top deck. Oh, and first he made her suck his cock, and she didn't look like she enjoyed it.

"Dinner's ready."

"I've lost my appetite."

Leo stepped into the room and crouched beside the chair I'd dragged up to the window. "Don't watch that. You're only hurting yourself."

"I'm beyond that. I'm dreaming up ways to hurt him."

"Come on, leave them to it and tell me about it over dinner."

"I told you—"

"Then sit with me while I eat. I'm still hungry."

He took me by the elbow and led me downstairs to the dining room. A twelve-seat table seemed overkill for the two of us, but it was better than sitting with our plates on our knees like we had been for the past few weeks.

And it turned out Leo really could cook. I thought he'd been kidding, but the homemade ravioli filled with minced salmon looked as good as anything I'd seen in a restaurant.

"Perhaps I'll just have a few mouthfuls."

"I knew you'd get tempted."

It tasted every bit as good as it smelled, so delicious I almost licked the plate. "Is there any more?"

"Sorry. But I can make it again tomorrow if you want?"

"I could eat that every day and never get sick of it."

"Do you cook?"

I choked a little. "Not anything you'd want to eat."

"I'm sure you're not that bad. Maybe I could help you out with some simple recipes?"

"You don't get it. My cooking'll kill you." And then I told him how I planned to take out Raul.

Only as with every plan, there was a flaw in it, and his name was Vadim. And after our excursion on board, he had eyes everywhere.

Back in the marina, he'd been relatively relaxed about security, but now he was wired. Every fifteen minutes, he'd patrol the edge of the boat, and in between, he'd sit out on deck or take a walk down the path that led to the front of the property they'd moored at. They still got their deliveries of flowers and sushi and groceries, thank goodness, but the delivery drivers weren't allowed near the boat anymore. Vadim met them by the gates and carried the bags and bouquets himself.

Even in the dark, things didn't get much better. Leo and I took it in turns to keep watch for a couple of nights, and Vadim popped up at odd hours smoking or drinking coffee.

The only time he left the boat at all was to go to the gym, and his number two guy sat on the swim platform in a deck chair until Vadim came back.

"What do we do?" Leo asked. "You need to get back on the boat again, don't you?"

"They're here for almost two more months. Let's give them a week and see if Vadim lowers his guard again."

"And in the meantime, you can get back in the water."

Terrific. I knew I needed to do it, but that didn't make the thought any more appealing.

"I'll do that tomorrow."

"How about today? We have that classy swimming pool out back. You can try that to start with."

"I'll consider it."

"I'm gonna use the gym. If you're not in the pool by the time I finish, I'll throw you in."

"You wouldn't."

He grinned as he walked towards the back of the house. "You really want to find out?"

I compromised and made it onto a sun lounger by the time a sweaty Leo walked onto the terrace. It seemed a shame not to get a tan while I was here, and I could keep an eye on *Liquidity* from behind my sunglasses. With a variety of plants impeding the view and another ugly hat, I wasn't worried about being recognised.

"What did I say?" Leo asked, standing over me.

"You weren't serious, were you?"

His answer was to pick me up and throw me over his shoulder. I almost took him to the deck, but I caught sight of Vadim looking in our direction and realised that would somewhat blow our cover. Hot-model girlfriends weren't supposed to be proficient in martial arts. Instead, I settled for shrieking a bit as Leo leapt into the deep end with me.

"You asshole!"

I clutched at the top of my string bikini as the thing threatened to lose its precarious grip on my breasts.

"I did warn you. No more putting things off."

I trod water, glaring at him. "I planned to get in later."

"No, you didn't. Come on, ten lengths and you can get out."

"Fine."

He was sort of right. Okay, entirely right. I hadn't planned to get in at all, and I couldn't keep putting things off. Ten lengths wouldn't take long.

And he swam beside me, keeping pace until I pulled myself onto the steps at the end.

"There, that wasn't so bad, was it?"

"I guess not. Although I still need to go in the sea."

"We can do that tomorrow. Maybe the day after if I'm feeling generous."

I reached out and traced his abs in an attempt to change the subject. "You're looking in better shape already."

"Yeah, I know. The gym in there isn't too bad, and I've been eating again." He jerked his thumb at the house. "I still can't believe this place, but I'm worried about what it's costing you."

"Don't. It's a gift from a friend."

Leo raised an eyebrow. "He must be a very good friend."

"She again. And renting this place is pocket change for her." Me as well, if I cared to admit it.

"Maybe I can thank her someday?"

"Maybe you can."

CHAPTER 18

TWO DAYS LATER, I lay out in the yard, pretending to read a book. With my phone next to me and Blackwood's finest keeping an eye on the boat, I could afford to close my eyes if I wanted to, but old habits died hard.

Last night, I'd crept into the yard under cover of darkness and positioned the cameras right where I needed them—one in a tree looking out over *Liquidity*'s stern, and another hidden inside a fake rock watching the bow.

Leo had looked on in fascination last night as I commandeered the kitchen to make the rock— homemade plastic was one of the first things I'd learned how to cook when I got my own apartment, and it was easier than you might think—heat eighteen ounces of milk until just below boiling point, add eight tablespoons of vinegar, stir, and run it through a strainer. The plastic stayed malleable enough to mould into a suitable blob around the camera lens, and then I pressed dirt into the surface as a disguise.

"Looks okay, doesn't it?" I asked Leo.

"Remind me never to get on your bad side."

"You'll stay on my good side if you make dinner again."

"Deal."

Now, Leo sprawled on the sun lounger next to me, only he genuinely was engrossed in his thriller novel. I cut my eyes to *Liquidity* once more—Vadim was still on deck, sipping a cup of what I assumed was coffee. After all, he spent long enough awake.

I had to admit, there were worse places to be on surveillance duty. The sun caressed us with its gentle rays, a light breeze kept us cool, and fragrant scents from the beautifully landscaped yard drifted over. Bougainvillaea, oleander, hibiscus, datura, daphne, adenium. My kind of garden.

In fact, I could have relaxed there until the sun went down if not for Leo and his insistence we go swimming.

"I've looked it up on the internet, and there's a secluded beach in Barker's National Park. That should suit us."

Great. At least there wouldn't be many people around to see me freak out. "Do we have to do this?"

He squeezed my hand. "You know we do."

In a walk-in cupboard next to the gym, the owner of the house had thoughtfully provided sporting equipment for every eventuality. Leo had gone through it with glee yesterday.

"Golf? Do you play golf?" he asked.

"I own a set of golf clubs."

"What's your handicap?"

"I don't know what a handicap is. I use them for hitting intruders."

"Oh. How about tennis? Do you play?"

"I tried it out for a few months." When I'd been hired to bump off a tennis-obsessed crook. "I soon got bored to death."

He rummaged again and held up a pair of cross-country skis. "Where do they think we're gonna use these? Oh, hey, what about badminton?"

Meanwhile, a set of snorkelling gear in the corner caught my eye, and I hauled out two pairs of fins, plus matching masks and snorkels. "These'll come in useful."

"So, you're gonna get back in the sea soon?"

"Looks like it."

And now Leo shovelled our swimming kits into a bag and herded me towards the car. Soon we were heading towards the protected acres of the national park.

"I thought it would be prettier than this," Leo said, as we drove in through faded gates. Litter marred the beauty of the vegetation either side of the gravel track.

"At least it's not busy."

We bumped over the potholes and headed for the coast, and wildlife gradually overcame the evidence of man's carelessness. Birds flitted from branch to branch, and the stark beauty of the mangroves gave an overriding impression of isolation. The beach itself stretched as far as we could see in either direction, empty white sand without another soul in sight.

"The website said not many people visit during the week."

I guess the lack of amenities put a lot of them off too. No stores, no restaurants, not even a bathroom. Good thing I was used to roughing it.

Leo stripped down to his trunks while I took off my T-shirt and shorts. At least with sitting around in the yard for so long, I'd gotten a nice tan. Leo too. And I couldn't help noticing those abs again. With all the crunches he'd been doing this week and the improvements in his diet, he'd started to gain even more definition. I forced my eyes upwards. But his roots needed doing.

He grabbed both pairs of fins and tossed me my mask and snorkel. "Ready?"

"No."

He ignored that, and I locked the car, hiding the keys beneath a nearby fallen tree. I took a deep breath. Ready? Not by a long shot.

Leo waded into the sea and turned to wait for me. For a moment, I was tempted to run away, but he'd probably catch up. I'd seen him on the treadmill, and he was faster than he looked. I dipped a toe into the water and shuddered.

"It's not that cold."

"I know."

I took another couple of steps, until the water came mid-thigh. Leo held out his hand, and I slipped mine into it. Why did this feel easier when he was with me?

The water lapped at my neck, and although it only came to Leo's chest, he tipped backwards.

"Float with me."

So I did, fins and mask trailing underwater in my hand, and life didn't seem so bad as I drifted under the blue sky, my fingers entwined with Leo's.

At least until he took the fins from me and slipped them on my feet. "Time to do some work."

"I'm only swimming today. No diving."

"We'll see."

I spat in my mask and rinsed it to prevent it fogging up, then slipped it over my face and flipped onto my front. Beside me, Leo did the same.

And I have to confess, watching his thighs rippling in the sunlight as he swam in front distracted me from the whole water thing. Before I knew it, he'd turned back to shore.

He slung an arm around my shoulders as we walked up the beach. "You did good. Head okay?" He tapped his temple with a finger.

I didn't dare confess what I'd been thinking about. After all, he'd told me I wasn't his type, and since that night outside the summerhouse, he hadn't shown the slightest interest in me sexually other than a bit of banter.

He said I was sexy, but clearly that wasn't enough for him.

Still, I couldn't help trying to catch a glimpse of his naked ass when he went behind the car to change. Seeing it in Mack's emailed photos was like being shown a picture of a puppy—cute, but all I really wanted to do was hold it in my own hands.

I rubbed myself down with a towel and put on dry clothes, trying to put naked Leo out of my mind. I'd already fucked this job up once due to wayward thoughts, and it mustn't, mustn't happen again.

When we got back to the villa, Vadim was still maintaining his vigil on deck, and according to the Blackwood surveillance team, he'd only stepped inside for five minutes in all the time we'd been gone. Honestly, it was getting beyond a joke. At this rate, two months would fly past and Raul would be back in Atlanta while Leo and I burned to a crisp in the sun.

My good mood evaporated as I stomped into the house.

"What's up?" Leo followed me into the living room.

"Fucking Vadim. He's screwing up my plans."

For two reasons. First, I needed to get onto the boat without being seen, and second, I didn't want him around to help Raul—prompt medical attention could save him. I hadn't flown over a thousand miles to Grand Cayman for the asshole to walk out of the hospital. I flopped onto one of the cream leather couches, all too aware I looked like a drama queen.

"I'll have to do something about him," I said.

"Like what?"

"Remove him from the equation."

"You mean kill him as well?"

"I'd rather not. Two deaths on one boat would look damned suspicious. I just need to stop him from watching everything."

Leo took the seat opposite. "How can you do that?"

I stared out of the window. Anybody might have thought I was looking for inspiration, but I was actually making a choice. Finally, my gaze settled on a green bush with pretty pink flowers.

"Oleander."

"Oleander?"

"Yes. Oleander."

"And what's that?"

I pointed. "*Nerium oleander*. Active ingredient oleandrin, a cardiac glycoside which interferes with the sodium-potassium ATPase pump in heart muscle cells. Basically, it makes the heart contract faster and more strongly than it should and throws off its rhythm. A high dose can cause seizures, coma, and death. Oh, and just to make it more fun, throw in sickness and diarrhoea."

Leo's eyes grew wider with every word. "I don't know whether to be impressed or run for the hills."

"We're on an island. There aren't any hills."

"Guess I'm impressed then. But how are you going to get Vadim to eat it?"

"That's the part I haven't worked out yet. It's bitter, so it'll need to go in something with a strong flavour."

"Coffee?"

"That would be perfect, but I need to get it into the damn coffee grounds and he rarely goes out. Just the occasional trip to a club with Raul and the gym." Hmm... The gym... Yes, that could actually work. "The gym. I need to find out what he drinks in the gym. If it's water, that's no good, but a sweet energy drink? Perfect."

"Why are you staring at me like that?"

"Because I need a little favour."

The next morning, I dropped Leo off a couple of streets away from Bud's Gym with a wedge of cash. According to the company's website, tourists could buy membership by the week or month, no joining fee required.

"Remember, you need to note down where the security cameras are," I reminded Leo.

"You already said that."

"And try not to talk to people."

"Got it."

"I wish there was another way to do this, but I can't

get into that gym unnoticed. It's full of men. With the changes to your hair and beard, I'm ninety-nine percent sure Vadim won't recognise you."

"What about the other one percent?"

"Dammit." I stomped on the brakes and brought the SUV to a stop at the side of the road. "We'll go back. I'll think of something else."

"Sasha, stop panicking." Leo reached over and flicked the turn signal on. "Drive to the gym. I'll be fine. If there's one thing I do know, it's how to work out. Stop worrying."

But I couldn't, and I didn't even know why. I never worried like this about Emmy when we worked together. But then again, Emmy knew how to look after herself.

I ran a few errands in town while I waited for Leo. Hair dye, donuts, that sort of thing. And worried. An hour passed, then two, and finally my phone buzzed.

"Can you pick me up?"

"You got the membership?"

"Yup, I got it."

Leo met me on the same side street where I'd left him and hopped into the car. I hoped his smile was a good sign.

"Took your time."

"I wasn't about to go to a gym without taking advantage of the weights."

Fair enough. Anything that contributed to those muscles had to be considered a plus point. "Did you see Vadim?"

"Not today, but I bench pressed two hundred pounds. I'll have to go back tomorrow."

CHAPTER 19

I KIND OF missed Leo when he wasn't around. There, I admitted it. He'd grown on me and gone from one of those annoying bits of lint you want to flick off to that comfy sweater you want to curl up in when you get home.

And he made me pancakes for breakfast.

But each morning, he drove off to the gym, leaving me alone in a house far too big for one person.

Not that I wasted the time. I used the little gym at the house, watched *Liquidity*, and sometimes I even braved the pool. Oh, and I finally found a use for that ski equipment.

"Can you buy me a bicycle inner tube?" I asked Leo on his way out one day.

"But you don't have a bike?"

"No, I'm making a pole spear."

"A what?"

"For fishing. Oh, and I need a tube of waterproof epoxy."

"Can't you just buy a spear thing?"

I shook my head. "Spear fishing's illegal in the Caymans unless you have a permit. And they only issue permits to residents. So if I want a ready-made spear, I'll either need to bribe someone who lives here to buy it for me or steal it. Much less risky to make it myself."

"And you know how?"

"I've done it before."

He nodded and smiled. "Why doesn't that surprise me?"

While he got to work on his body, I hauled the treasures I'd found into the kitchen. The ski pole. A bamboo cane from the yard. An eye-bolt and hacksaw from the shelf in the garage, duct tape and zip ties from the drawer in the utility room, and the paracord I always carried in my own luggage.

By the time Leo came back, apart from a dab of glue on each end and the rubber sling I needed to fire the thing, I had my spear.

He took a seat at the breakfast bar and watched as I finished. First, I tied knots in a short piece of paracord and wedged them into the inner tube, then secured them with zip ties either side of the knots. I looped that around the eye-bolt I'd screwed into the cane and wedged into the larger end of the ski pole, then added a blob of glue to hold in the prongs I'd fashioned from a coat hanger at the other end.

"Done."

"You can really catch a fish with that?"

"I had plenty of practice when I lived by the sea in Vietnam. I used to catch something for dinner most days."

"You dived that often?"

I stared out the window at the yacht moored beyond. "Raul broke me."

Dammit. I hadn't gotten sniffly for ages, and now the tears welled up again. Would this ever pass?

Leo gathered me up in his arms and held me to his chest. "And I'll try to make you whole again."

He kissed my hair as I sobbed into his chest, all the while feeling mortified I'd cracked yet again. I needed more than a tube of epoxy to stick myself back together.

I needed Raul's fucking blood.

Pull yourself together, Fia. I forced myself to stop blubbing and straightened up. "Any sign of Vadim in the gym?"

"Yeah, he came in today. The man's a damn machine. He benches three-fifty."

"And lives on coffee and steroids."

"And orange Gatorade."

Hallelujah! Everyone had a favourite flavour, and I hoped he stuck to it. "Fingers crossed he's drinking it again tomorrow."

"I saw him buy it out the vending machine, and they only sell Orange and Cool Blue."

For the first time since the night we dived off the boat, I relaxed a little inside. We could pull this thing off. We had to.

When we headed to Barker's beach the next day, I felt more positive than I had in ages. As I lay in bed last night, I'd even thought back to my old life by the water, with nothing but me, the sun, and the sea.

I'd taken a few months off to recharge after a particularly gruelling couple of years—nine kills in twenty-five months. My bank balance had been in good stead, but my sanity hung on by a thread.

Back then, water had healed me. Today, it had become my enemy. H_2O. Essential for life but so easy to die in.

Today, I waded into the sea ahead of Leo. He held up my mask and fins.

"Don't you need these?"

"I only need myself today."

Before I could back out, I dove under, swimming among the fish and the coral like I used to do. A pair of creole wrasses darted out of my way while a goatfish dug through the sand on the bottom. I used my feet to kick down, past a southern stingray resting on the bottom, and disturbed a colony of tube worms who popped their feathered ends back inside as I drew close. And all the time, I kept my eyes open for the prize.

Leo was scanning the waves when I surfaced, and he quickly stroked towards me.

"You had me worried. I thought you weren't gonna come up."

"I'd forgotten how beautiful it could be down there."

"You took your time finding that out. How long can you stay under?"

"A minute easily. Two, if I take it slow." I dropped my voice. "Three or four if my life's in danger."

He gave my hand a squeeze. "Let's stick with one today, okay? My heart won't take any more."

I still felt a tightness in my chest every time I sank beneath the water, but it got easier. At least, until the afternoon. We'd swum half a mile from the car by then, following the underwater beauty of the coral pinnacles just offshore, me diving and Leo snorkelling on the surface.

"You look so graceful down there," he said after one particularly long dive. "You need a mermaid tail."

Aw, he was being sweet.

He mimed holding his chest. "And one of those clamshell bras."

Okay, now he was being a prick. I reached out and poked him in the stomach, but after his days in the gym, it was like stubbing my finger on a brick wall.

"You're gonna pay for that," he growled.

"No way."

I ducked under the water, heading away from Leo. Then something tugged at my legs, and suddenly I hurtled off into the blue. Leo got smaller and smaller as I tried to kick back to him. The current was stronger than me, and I couldn't fight it. The night under the bridge flooded back to me as I stared death in the face again, only this time it wasn't Raul's face I saw. It was Leo's.

And I imagined his voice, soothing me, calming me, telling me what to do as the water tore me farther from the shore.

"Don't fight it. Kick to the surface."

By then, I didn't even know which way was up. Just blue, blue, all around. I let a dribble of my precious air trickle out between my lips, and as the bubbles floated towards the surface, I pulled myself after them.

I broke the surface gasping, still being towed out to sea, but now I recognised the riptide and swam parallel to the beach until I broke free of its deadly grip.

But where was Leo?

Please say he didn't get caught in it too.

Then I spotted his lime green snorkel a quarter of a mile in the distance, bobbing above the ripples, and I swam towards it.

"Sasha!" he yelled, when he caught sight of me.

"I'm okay."

We reached each other a minute later, and I flung my arms around him. Then twined my legs around his waist for good measure.

"Fuck." He laid his forehead against mine. "I thought I'd lost you."

I didn't want to let on how terrified I'd been. "I'm fine."

"I've never seen a current like that."

"Me neither."

The closest I'd come was with Emmy in Thailand, but we'd been younger and more daring in those days, and once we got out, we'd circled around again for another turn.

Today? I just felt drained.

"Shall we call it a day?" he asked.

"We haven't got the fish."

"We can get the damn fish tomorrow. Right now, I want to take you home and make you lunch."

I gave him a small smile. "Okay."

The incident with the riptide shook me up more than I let on. I tried to hide my trembles as I wrapped the towel around myself, but Leo noticed anyway. I was still standing by the side of the car once he'd changed his shorts.

"Come here." He pulled me into a hug. "You're amazing; did anyone ever tell you that?"

"No."

"Come on, your parents must have."

"My mother abandoned me when I was four years

old, and my daddy was pure evil."

"At least he was there for you."

"Believe me, I'd much rather he hadn't been."

"He didn't hit you, did he?"

"Only once."

"Then what was so bad? Evil's a strong word."

I stayed silent, but Leo guessed. I saw it in his eyes, the pity brimming out of them as he took my hand. "He didn't... Tell me he didn't touch you like that."

"I could tell you, but I'd be lying." The voice that spoke wasn't mine. "He was always so gentle. So *loving*. Sometimes it felt uncomfortable, but he'd stroke my hair and tell me it was okay, that he understood and we'd take things slow. I thought it was normal until I overheard girls talking at school and realised it was anything but."

Leo's fingers dug into my arm, but I relished the pain. His mouth set in a hard line.

"I'll kill him. No man should touch a child like that."

"There's no need."

"But... Oh, shit." Leo closed his eyes and leaned against the car. "Tell me you didn't..."

"Back then, the only person I could depend on was myself. I got too old for him, and he married some woman who was dumb as shit. She had a four-year-old daughter. Four. Years. Old. I saw the way my daddy looked at that little girl."

"I hate that you had to go through that."

"Can we just not talk about it? I don't even like to *think* about it." Every time I did, the anger simmered in my veins, a distraction I didn't need. Not with my career as a cold-blooded killer.

My tone made him back off. "Okay, I won't push you. But I'm here if you ever need to talk."

"I won't."

A flicker of hurt crossed his face, and then he sighed. "Better get you dressed."

He held up my T-shirt for me to put my arms in, like I was a small child.

"I'm all wet."

"Doesn't matter." He tugged it on, and once the hem settled at my waist, he reached under and untied my bikini top. "There."

Then he did the same with the shorts, leaving me commando. The seam of my shorts rubbed between my legs, and that, together with the memory of his hands on me, stoked the fire in my belly. For the first time ever, I longed to touch myself to relieve the ache. But in the car next to Leo? No way. I kept my hands firmly on my thighs as we bounced over the potholes in the direction of our villa.

He kept his word when we got back and made me pizza for lunch. The delicious, cheesy goodness had the power to heal a thousand aches and even helped to soothe my troubled thoughts. By the time I'd overdosed on calories, I felt almost human again.

And I needed to practise with my spear. That damned ocean wasn't going to defeat me. Leo sat on a fancy chaise longue and watched me as I fired the improvised weapon into a cardboard box in the hallway, time after time until it became second nature. Wrap the inner tube around my hand between my thumb and forefinger. Slide the pole through my hand until the rubber reached maximum tension. Aim. Release. By late evening, I hit the centre of the box with every shot.

"I'm impressed. Who knew you could do that with a ski pole?"

"We still need to find a puffer fish. I saw two today, but one was too small and the other was off in the distance."

"At least we know they're around. Will you be up to going out tomorrow?"

"Damn right I will."

Three times water had tried to kill me, and three times it failed. I was determined it wouldn't get a fourth opportunity.

CHAPTER 20

MY RINGING PHONE woke me the next morning, and I glared at the screen. I'd been having a nice dream about L... No, no I hadn't.

I snatched up the phone and jabbed the answer button. "Emmy?"

"Still sleeping alone?"

"I told you I would be."

"Damn. Okay, it's Monday. My day in the pool is Saturday. We've still got time."

"I keep telling you..."

"Yeah, yeah. Anyway, Mack finally got into that data. It's fucking gold. The Ice Cream Man's gonna cream his pants."

"You realise how terrible that line sounded?"

"Hmm, I suppose. Seeing as he's ice cream, he'd more melt in them."

"That's sick."

"Not if it's mint choc chip." Emmy's favourite flavour.

But not mine. "Ugh."

Mint Choc Chip had been fourth on the list. A flabby banker for an organised crime syndicate, he'd died from an overdose of the coke he liked to snort in his spare time. Inhaling pure rather than cut powder would do that to a guy. Shame. And I'd had to watch while he flopped around like a beached beluga, talking to himself until his heart gave out.

"Can we talk about something other than ice cream?"

"You back in the sea yet?"

"I got sucked away by a riptide yesterday."

"What a rush. Hey, you wanna take a surfing break when you get back?"

"No, I want to find a mountain in Death Valley and build a house there."

Emmy burst into laughter. "I'm glad things are going so well."

My voice dropped. "I need to get back in the water today for that damned puffer."

"And you will. It's almost over, honey. You're halfway there."

"A third. I need to get through Vadim to take out Raul." I explained about the plans with the oleander.

"It's always a tragedy when a guy over-exerts himself in the gym, isn't it?"

"That's what I'm hoping for. I've got to go. I need to find a fish."

"Bye, honey. Don't forget—Saturday."

With her voice still echoing in my ears, apart from the Saturday comment, which I blocked out entirely, I knocked on Leo's door.

"I'm asleep."

I pushed it open and found him still in bed. Shirtless. My heart sped up, and I raised my voice to cover the pounding in my chest.

"Can we get an early start? I want to get the diving over with."

"Give me five minutes to throw some clothes on?"

"Meet you downstairs."

While he changed, I grabbed a couple of pieces of fruit, carefully avoiding the apple I'd hidden the memory stick in the centre of. I didn't want to break a tooth. By the time Leo came downstairs, I'd made smoothies and thrown our gear in the car. The spear itself was hidden in the trunk, under a picnic blanket and the badminton set from the equipment room.

Leo picked up his drink and sniffed it. "I'm nervous of anything you make now."

"Don't be. If I wanted you dead, you would be already."

"That's hardly a comforting thought."

I sidled a little closer. "I don't want you dead. I suck at making my own pancakes."

He slid an arm around my waist and grinned. "Is there anything else you suck at?"

I shoved him away. "Ugh! Men."

But I couldn't help glancing down. Yeah, I would. I totally would.

Early morning, and as usual our stretch of Barker's beach was deserted. One day, they'd build amenities—beach huts, cafés, kiddy playgrounds—and the tourists would come, but for now I enjoyed its unspoilt beauty.

And the gifts it could offer me.

I started off with the mask and snorkel that day, and Leo and I swam side-by-side, hunting for our quarry.

Puffer fish aren't particularly fast swimmers. They don't need to be because they have other defence mechanisms, namely the ability to turn themselves into a spiky soccer ball and a liver that's poisonous as fuck. Guess which of those I planned to utilise?

But first I needed to catch one.

We'd been swimming for an hour when I saw it. A two-foot-long spotted puffer, resting under a clump of coral. I felt a pang of guilt at killing such a majestic creature, but its sacrifice would lead to lives being saved, starting with the secretary's most likely. If the argument we'd heard about Raul's other woman was any indication, I bet he planned to leave the Caymans with pneumatic Barbie and arrive in Atlanta alone.

I swam closer, and the fish flickered a lazy eye. Their eyesight was excellent, and although they usually moved slowly, the species was capable of a relatively uncontrolled burst of speed if it felt threatened.

From the edge of my vision, I saw Leo and motioned at him to keep back. The fish didn't move.

I drew back the spear, praying my target practice paid off, knowing that it would. Deep in the hunt, everything came back to me. The tightening in my chest as I approached my prey. The way my vision sharpened. The way nothing else mattered.

I aimed.

Fired.

Hit it dead centre.

The fish struggled on the end of the barbed pole, and I unclipped the knife from the waistband of my bikini to put it out of its misery. One quick twist in its brain stem and the creature lay dead.

I wouldn't be so kind with Raul.

Leo and I both wore gloves today as in some cases puffer fish could have poisonous skin. Between us, we carried the beast into the trunk and wrapped it in the picnic blanket. The sun blinked through the whispering trees and rippled on the azure water as we drove away from Barker's beach for the last time. Goodbye, paradise.

I almost felt sad to be leaving.

"Kitchen's mine for the rest of the day," I told Leo. "We'll have to get takeout."

"After you've done your thing, I'm not sure I ever want to eat in there again."

"Relax, I'll clean up. It's not my first rodeo."

And I sure as hell knew what to do with a filleting knife. By early afternoon I'd got all the bits I wanted, covered in saran wrap on a tray and ready to go into the freezer.

"Fugu?"

I held up a piece of the leftover pufferfish to Leo as he came to check on me.

"I thought you said you weren't trying to kill me?"

"The flesh is safe enough."

I popped the thin sliver into my own mouth, chewed, and swallowed.

"You're crazy."

"Would you want me any other way?"

"No." He shook his head, and his throat bobbed as he swallowed. "I want you exactly as you are."

Why had the temperature in the room suddenly risen a couple of notches? I fanned myself with my hand. "Well, better get on with the next part."

I hurried out to the oleander bushes, leaving Leo

and his perplexity inside. I needed to do some yardwork.

CHAPTER 21

THIS WAS FAR worse than the first day I'd driven Leo to the gym. Today, he had two bottles full of deadly Gatorade, one orange, one blue, and I had a whole lot of expectations.

Vadim had bought that drink every day he'd been at the gym. But what if he didn't today? Or what if someone saw Leo swap the bottles over? Or I'd got the dose wrong? Or he decided he wasn't thirsty and threw it away?

I gripped the wheel and forced myself to take a few deep breaths. If Vadim didn't drink the poison today, we could come back tomorrow. The only thing that mattered was Leo getting out safely.

To stop myself from going mad, I parked and studied my shopping list. While Leo dealt with Vadim, I needed to make preparations for Raul. First on the list were sticky labels, a printer, and clear tape. The graphics department at Blackwood had mocked me up a label for my deadly box of sushi, but I needed to print it out.

The box itself would be recycled. The blurb on Love Sushi's website said they sold their upmarket selections at various grocers on the island, and over the past couple of weeks, Leo and I had sampled most of their offerings. We had the leftover packaging to prove it.

According to the order schedule Mack had lifted from Love Sushi's computer system, Raul was a creature of habit. Every day, he got the deluxe box delivered—six futomaki, six uramaki, two nigiri, a generous helping of sashimi, and a couple of gunkan served up with pickled ginger, wasabi, and tiny bottles of soy sauce.

"It's been the same since he came to the island," she said. "I'll keep an eye out and tell you if it changes."

"I feel kind of bad the sushi company might get investigated over this."

"Don't. They might have fancy boxes and a glossy website, but they've also been written up four times in the last year for hygiene violations. The Department of Environmental Health has been looking for an excuse to close them down."

"Thanks. I ate their food for lunch yesterday."

"Might I suggest sticking to Burger King?"

I'd stick with Leo's cooking, thanks.

We'd bought sushi rice, seaweed, fish and vegetables, and between us, Leo and I had spent the past week learning how to prepare passable imitations. And with the fresh boxes I'd buy today, we'd be able to reuse some of the ingredients as well as the condiments. We even had the plastic chopsticks with the logo on them.

But first, we needed to get Vadim out of the way. What was Leo doing?

By midday, I'd rounded up the packaging and ingredients and made it back to the car. Poisoning someone was so much more difficult when you subbed the job out. Was this how the Ice Cream Man felt? Did he sit in his office in Langley, drumming his fingertips on the table and popping antacids?

The distant sound of a siren made me look up. Where was it coming from? Police, ambulance, or fire?

Please, not the police.

I checked my phone for the hundredth time as the ambulance sped past in the direction of the gym. Where was Leo? Why hadn't he called?

Time seemed to slow as I waited, and I'd begun to experience some symptoms of oleander poisoning myself—the pounding heart, the dizziness, the feeling of nausea.

Then my phone buzzed. I snatched it up.

"Can you come and get me?"

"Two minutes."

Leo was waiting around the corner from the gym when I arrived, and he climbed in the car and stripped off his neoprene weightlifting gloves. I looked around, but there was no ambulance in sight.

"How'd it go?"

He leaned back in the seat and closed his eyes, then a slow smile spread over his face.

"Smooth as a gallon of buttermilk going through a hound dog."

I shrieked and flung myself at him, then remembered I didn't do that kind of thing and tried to push myself back to the driver's side. But Leo held onto me.

"Sasha, you scare me more every day."

"I'm not sure whether to take that as a compliment or not?"

He thought for a second. "In your line of work, I guess you should."

I'd never explicitly told Leo what I did for a living,

but I'd not exactly hidden it either. And he hadn't run for the hills. That was a good sign.

"So, what happened?"

He pointed at the road. "I'll tell you as we drive."

I started the engine and pulled away, desperate to hear of Vadim's fate. How badly had we hurt him?

"Vadim visited the john halfway through his workout, and I followed him into the locker room. No security cameras in there. He left his bottle of Gatorade on the bench, and I swapped them over. He'd only taken a mouthful by then."

Vadim drank virtually the full bottle? This got better and better. "He got sick in the gym?"

"He tried to bench press three-seventy, but everyone could see it was a strain. A bunch of guys were watching him. Then he threw up, clutched at his chest, and fell right off the bench."

"And it couldn't have happened to a nicer guy."

"Someone called an ambulance, and I couldn't resist sticking around. I'm pretty sure he had a heart attack. Fuck, I can't believe I just did that."

"That's the best news I've had all year."

"It gets even better. I got the bottle back." Leo reached into his gym bag and held it up, the orange flavour. "A quarter left. And no, that weight bench isn't covered by cameras either."

I shrieked again. I couldn't help it. Fucking hell, I'd turned into new Emmy. Old Emmy, the ice queen, would have nodded and muttered "Good." New Emmy, after all her own dramas, had developed one hell of a squeal. And now I'd freaking caught it.

I tried to act with a little more decorum. "I mean, that's good news."

Leo managed a smile, but when he buckled the seatbelt, I noticed his hands were shaking.

"I preferred the shriek," he muttered.

Liquidity was a hive of activity when we arrived back. Raul paced the deck on the phone while the captain, the deckhand, and Vadim's assistant looked on anxiously. Only the secretary looked bored, lying on a sun lounger with a magazine.

I peered out the kitchen window. "Looks as if they've heard the news. Wonder what Raul's gonna do?"

The answer was get in a taxi with Vadim's shadow and speed off, presumably to the hospital. It would have been a perfect moment to sneak onto the boat, but today's sushi delivery hadn't arrived yet.

We needed to wait.

I called Mack and asked her to check on Vadim's condition. Half an hour later she confirmed Leo's suspicions—Vadim had suffered a heart attack, and the doctors were trying to stabilise him. Apparently, they'd had to restart him twice already. I couldn't help hoping it would be third time unlucky.

"Are you ready to make sushi?" I asked Leo.

"I need a glass of wine first. How do you do it?"

"Do what?"

"Act so casually about all this. I mean, Vadim's not even dead, and look."

He held out a hand. Yup, still shaking.

"Practice?" Inside, I was buzzed, and the casual exterior was a look I'd perfected over the years.

"I don't think I wanted to hear that."

I shrugged. "Maybe I'm just a psychopath."

"That's not any better."

I fetched a bottle of white from the fridge and poured Leo a generous glassful. "Here, try this. It's time to cook."

Darkness fell, but my adrenalin levels didn't. In the refrigerator sat a perfect box of sushi, a special selection with fugu uramaki and half a dozen slices of puffer fish sashimi. Tomorrow, I'd deliver it.

And tonight, I couldn't sleep. It wasn't the first time on a job I hadn't been able to. As the moon hovered high in the sky, I paced the house, stopping at each window in turn to look at *Liquidity*, bobbing gently at her mooring.

"Why aren't you in bed?" Leo's voice came from the kitchen doorway.

"Insomnia."

"You need to get some rest. You've got a big day tomorrow."

"I know, but tell that to my brain. It's overthinking everything."

"Have you tried meditation?"

"Once. It didn't work."

"You need to try it more than once."

"I couldn't. The CD irritated me and I threw it out the window."

The vibrations of Leo's deep chuckle tickled my soul. "Then let's try something else. I have an idea."

"What idea?"

He didn't answer, just picked me up and started for the stairs. If he'd done that a few weeks ago, I'd have knocked him out, but now? I stayed still in his arms. "Where are we going?"

"It's a surprise."

"I don't like surprises."

"Trust me."

He laid me down on my bed. "Did I mention I'm also a qualified sports massage therapist?"

I sat up. "You're gonna give me a massage?"

"I guarantee you'll sleep afterwards. Now, take off your top and lie on your front. I need to find some lotion or something."

Leo's hands, all over me? The coals in my belly started to smoulder, and for a second I considered jumping into the swimming pool to cool off. But logic took over, and I remembered I'd always loved the heat. I peeled my top off and did as he asked.

He didn't take long to come back, and cold drops of moisturiser fell on my back. I shivered, but the drops were soon followed by warm hands.

"Tell me if the pressure gets too much," he said, pressing his thumbs either side of my spine.

The pressure on my back was just fine, but between my legs? I felt like I was about to explode. I clenched my thighs together to try and relieve the ache, but that only made things worse. Leo seemed oblivious as he kneaded my shoulders, digging out all the knots in my muscles. Fuck me, the man had magic fingers.

Then he stopped. "Better?"

"Can't. Speak."

"That means the answer's yes." Warm breath whispered over my skin as he tucked the duvet around me. "I'll see you in the morning." Then, more softly, "Good night, amazing girl."

The second the door clicked behind him, I buried my face in the pillow, reached inside my panties, and let go.

CHAPTER 22

THE ALARM WOKE me at six. I cursed and knocked it off the nightstand because I'd been having a delicious dream. Leo gave me a massage, and it felt so good I... Oh, wait. No, that actually happened.

I dragged myself into the shower to try and wake myself up, which didn't work. I needed another massage followed by eighteen hours of sleep, then I might feel halfway human. But today I didn't have that luxury. I had a job to do.

And the first thing I did was check in with Mack. I knew from experience she barely slept either. "Any news?"

"Vadim's in the ICU. Still alive, unfortunately."

"When are visiting hours?"

"Nine to eleven and four to eight."

If Raul chose to go to the hospital early, I could replace his lunch. I'd kept an eye out, and he hadn't eaten yesterday's box yet. If he picked the later slot, I'd replace the afternoon sushi delivery, and he'd get his fugu for lunch tomorrow. Either way would work, but I couldn't help hoping he'd go out in the morning. I didn't relish the idea of another sleepless night.

At half past eight, I stationed myself at the window, waiting for any signs of movement. Nothing. Nine o'clock came and went, then ten, and Raul emerged on deck with a mug and the newspaper. Heartless bastard.

"At least it's not just his girlfriends he couldn't give a shit about," I said. "Good to know he values Vadim as well."

Leo leaned back against the breakfast bar. "You know how important a good coffee is."

"I hope he's not heartless enough to skip visiting altogether."

"Nah, he'll need to find out when Vadim's coming back. Heaven forbid he might have to do his own dirty work."

I'd begun to worry about wearing a hole in the kitchen floor with my pacing by the time Raul stepped off the boat at half past three. The deckhand had taken delivery of the day's sushi twenty minutes earlier, and I'd checked on the box in my own refrigerator half a dozen times.

"It's still there," Leo said. "Don't worry, I haven't eaten it."

"I never used to get stressed like this. It's Raul. He's driven me to it."

Leo snagged me by the waist and pulled me against him. "That's because it's personal. You'll be fine for the next job, I'm sure of it."

"I don't know if I can carry on. My head's a mess. I'm thinking of retiring."

"How old are you?"

"Thirty."

He let out a low whistle. "Most people dream of retiring at thirty."

"Most people haven't lived a lifetime of shit at thirty."

"Then you'll have to make the next few decades

count."

I caught a shadow on the deck of *Liquidity*. "Hey! Raul's on the move."

"Then I guess we are too." He squeezed my hand. "I'd wish you luck, but you don't need it. I know you can pull this off."

"We. This is a team effort. I couldn't have gotten this far without you."

"And without you, I'd be in jail or dead."

I used a tea towel to pull the box of sushi out the refrigerator and slip it in a tote bag. "We can celebrate when Raul's in the morgue."

"I'll drink to that."

I rarely bothered with a disguise. Wigs itched and bits of latex stuck all over my face made me sweat. I'd always preferred to simply avoid leaving witnesses. My victims ended up dead, and I moved around carefully, so that didn't usually cause me a problem.

But today, walking into a hornet's nest in broad daylight? I took precautions. When I'd first come to the island, I picked up a couple of wigs, just in case, and today I selected a startling red one. I was working on the same theory as with the T-shirt. If someone saw me, they'd remember the hair and not a lot else. I topped it off with Leo's spare pair of glasses, although they slipped down my nose a bit. That didn't matter—if all went according to plan, I'd only be wearing them for a few minutes.

There was no point in skulking about in the bushes in broad daylight. Someone would only see me and call the cops. Instead, without the watchful eyes of Vadim on me, I sauntered through the side gate of the house next door but one and headed for *Liquidity*'s mooring. If anyone stopped me, I'd just apologise for getting the wrong house.

A hideous clump of pampas grass stood between me and the boat, its tough blades rustling in the breeze. To my left, I glimpsed Leo on our dock, shoving the canoe we'd found in the garage towards the edge. He'd never been in one before, which suited our plan perfectly.

A minute ticked past as he wrestled the thing into the water, and I closed my eyes as he climbed in. The canoe was wobbling everywhere, and I didn't want him to fall out. Yet.

With the clumsy strokes of a complete beginner, he paddled away from the side, and his call of, "See you later, honey," added a particularly nice touch.

I caught the captain watching him out of the salon window and smiled to myself. With the secretary sunning herself on the foredeck, the only person left unaccounted for was the deckhand. I could deal with that.

With perfect timing, Leo rounded the bow and overbalanced. The resulting splash was a thing to behold, and the secretary's shriek pierced the air as water covered her.

"You idiot! I'm soaked!"

Leo floundered about like a drowning man, and the captain ran towards him, pausing only to grab a life ring. I thought I detected a slight smirk when he passed the secretary. Then the deckhand sprinted out to help, and we were three for three.

I slipped from my hiding place and leapt onto the swim platform. The galley was at the rear of the salon, and that was where I needed to go. I made it in there and yanked open the refrigerator door. Sushi. Where was the damn sushi? I rifled through and found all sorts of other fish, fresh from the market. Good, that would help confuse things. But the sushi? Ah, there it was, in the crisper drawer. Who kept sushi in the crisper drawer? Mind you, I kept M&Ms in mine, so I figured I couldn't comment.

I shoved the old box in my tote bag and pulled out the fugu deluxe. I'd just had time to slide it in the drawer and close the door when I heard footsteps in the salon. A cupboard door opened and closed. A muttered curse.

Shit. The fucking secretary. I glanced around for a hiding place, but there was nowhere, not unless I could fold myself into a two-foot high cupboard.

I raised my eyes skywards. Please, don't come in here.

But of course, nobody listened.

She stood in the doorway with a hand on one hip. "Who the hell are you?"

Oh, fuck.

Now what? Did I come clean and tell her Raul tried to kill me? Explain that she'd most likely be next? Or try for an excuse?

She swayed a little and clutched at the door frame for support. Could it be? Yes! She was drunk. At four in the afternoon, she was utterly slaughtered. When she exhaled, I could smell the gin on her breath.

"I'm from the grocery delivery service. Usually, there's a guy here to meet me, but I can't find him, so I just put the stuff away."

"Vadim?"

"Yeah, that's him."

"He's in...hic...hoshpital. Did you bring more wine?"

Thankfully, I knew where Raul kept his stash. "Sure did. You want me to pour you a glass?"

"Yesh, pleash."

"Red or white?" Could she even tell the difference?

"White."

I carefully selected a nice expensive bottle, the $250 Domaine Leflaive Raul had been saving for a special occasion, and unscrewed the cork. How was the bitch still standing? I poured her a nice big glass and handed it over. She didn't bother to ask why I was wearing leather gloves in the heat.

"Thanksh."

She attempted a smile, but she couldn't focus properly.

"My pleasure. Enjoy your day."

She teetered off back outside, and I rolled my eyes. With any luck, even if she did remember me Raul would write it off as a drunken hallucination. Probably he wouldn't be too happy about the Domaine Leflaive either.

Voices drifted down the side gangway while I stood on the swim platform, and as they came closer, I shoved the wig and glasses into the tote bag, zipped it up, and slipped into the water. My last swim of the trip and I'd actually quite enjoy this one.

Chapter 23

"STOP FRETTING," LEO said.

I looked out the window for the hundredth time since I got back. Leo had arrived at the house before me, thanks to help from *Liquidity*'s crew.

"I can't. What if he doesn't eat the sushi? What if somebody else does?"

"Then we try again. Something different. We won't give up."

"This is the worst part. The waiting. I used to quite enjoy it. You know, the anticipation? But now I'm thinking I should have gone with a gun or a knife."

Leo herded me out of the kitchen. "Go and pack. That'll take your mind off things. With any luck, we'll be out of here tomorrow."

"You need to pack too."

"I'm already packed. I only have one bag. You have girl shit all over the bathroom, and who knows where you've hidden your goodies?"

Fair enough, he did have a point there. I needed to retrieve my knives from the spare bedroom and take a shower. "Okay, I'll pack. We need to take a drive and dump a few bits later as well."

I felt kind of sad to be saying goodbye to the house because despite the stress and the underlying reason I'd come here, sharing the space with Leo hadn't been entirely unpleasant. Apart from Raul, I'd never spent so much time with a guy, and now I could see what had been lacking in the former relationship. Trust. Laughter. Friendship. I thought I'd loved Raul when all I'd really liked was his dick.

Leo and I hadn't really spoken about the future, about what we'd do when we arrived back stateside. I'd threatened to retire, but I wasn't sure I could go through with it. I'd be bored for one thing. Three months in Vietnam taught me I wasn't designed for sitting on the beach permanently. The idea of Blackwood tempted me, but I'd take a vacation first.

But whatever happened, I wanted to help Leo financially if nothing else. If Raul died tomorrow, I'd get $3 million, plus expenses. Leo deserved a chunk of that, as long as his stupid male pride didn't get in the way.

Meanwhile, I loaded the trash into the car. A printer. A broken spear that had done its job. Half a dead fish. A Gatorade bottle. The pestle and mortar I'd used to grind the oleander. All the remnants of another chapter in my long and creepy career.

"Ready to go?"

Leo looked up from his spot at the kitchen counter. "Sure. And, no, there's no activity at the boat yet."

We drove halfway across the island, dropping trash into various dumpsters as we went. Leo chattered about the sights, comparing George Town to Governors Creek, and contemplating the restaurants that lined Seven Mile Beach.

"Shame we didn't get to see more of the island."

I gritted my teeth. "Never mix business with pleasure. I tried that once. Didn't work."

He reached over and pulled my spare hand into his lap. "I'm sorry it ever came to that. Maybe you can take a proper vacation when this is over?"

"I intend to. What about you? What will you do?"

"I haven't thought that far ahead. When I came here, I didn't think I'd be leaving."

"You'll go back to Atlanta, though?"

"I don't know. There's nothing left for me there, and it holds so many bad memories."

"You can make new ones. Good ones."

"I hope so."

I turned the car into the driveway and hit the garage door opener for most likely the final time. With the vehicle stopped, I had a chance to look at Leo. So fucking handsome, but that wasn't all. They say beauty's skin deep, but Leo's went the whole way through. He'd changed since I met him. He'd become more confident, supportive, caring. A true friend. The man you spend your whole life looking for.

I'd changed too. I'd walked to the edge of my sanity, and he'd helped me find my way back. I'd laughed. I'd cried. I'd loved. And I'd lost.

Because I wasn't his fucking type.

"I started dinner. Chicken. No fish," he said.

"Great."

"Sasha, don't stress about this."

I slammed the car door. "I can't help it."

He climbed out and stood in front of me. Close, but not touching. "You want me to take your mind off things again?"

A massage? The chance to have his hands all over me one last time? I had to take it. "Yes," I whispered.

I half expected him to pick me up like last night, but

he didn't.

"Turn around." His voice was lower. Huskier.

My eyes popped open. "Huh?"

"Turn around, Sasha. Face the car."

"What? Why?"

"Just. Do. It."

This was a side of Leo I hadn't seen before. I gave an involuntary shiver. Did he scare me? No, because I knew I could take him to the ground in a second. But he did do something else. That same rush I got from him last night shot south, and the flames inside me roared.

I turned.

"Hands on top of the car."

I complied.

Then my ass blazed as his hand came down on it.

"What the fuck was that for?"

He pressed the length of his body against me, and I could feel him hard already. His lips brushed my ear. "Because, gorgeous girl, you like a little pain with your pleasure. And tonight, you're gonna get it."

Holy hell, someone hand me a fire extinguisher. "I thought you said I wasn't your type?"

"Until I met you, I didn't even know I had a type."

"Then why did you tell me that?"

"You said it yourself earlier. Business before pleasure. And this afternoon, we finished the business."

He ran his hands down my arms, meshed his fingers in mine and squeezed hard. "Tell me to stop and I will, but I promise you'll enjoy this."

I lay my head back on his shoulder and groaned. "Do your worst."

He kicked my legs apart and I lurched forward,

slamming into the side of the car. I didn't get time for a breath before his hand stung my ass again. Of fuck, I shouldn't be enjoying this, but it felt so damn good.

Ripping sounds tore through the air as he shredded my clothes, then his slaps rained onto my bare skin. Soft, hard, everything in between. My stomach clenched, and I felt my juices trickling down my thighs.

I closed my eyes and gave in to the sensations. I should have been horrified. I should have been embarrassed, standing there starkers with my breasts pressed against a car window, about to come because a guy who made Scott Eastwood look ugly was abusing my ass. But I put all that out of my mind and just *felt* instead.

Who cared what anyone else might think? This was between Leo and me, and I loved it.

He leaned forward once more, skin to skin. He'd lost his shirt somewhere along the way.

"I can smell you from here, Sasha." He ran a finger between my legs. "I told you you'd like it."

"Fia."

"What? Fear?" He stepped back. "You're scared? Am I hurting you?" He sounded horrified.

"No, Fia. My name. Sofia. Not Sasha. Sofia."

His warmth returned, pressed against me. "Fia? It suits you better. I always wondered whether you'd told me the truth about that."

"Are you upset?"

"How could I be upset now? I'm about to fuck the most beautiful woman I've ever met."

He slid a couple of fingers inside, making me gasp. I ground down on them shamelessly, desperate for some relief. And he fucking laughed.

"Patience, gorgeous. Not yet."

His other hand came to my front and cupped a breast. I waited for him to work his magic with my nipple, and I wasn't disappointed.

"Yes yet."

"Wait."

His fingers moved forward and circled my jewel with agonising slowness. This wasn't fun anymore. If he didn't hurry up, I'd self-combust.

"Your ass is beautifully pink."

"It'll be beautifully annoyed if you don't let me come."

"Feisty. I never knew I'd fall for a feisty woman."

I stilled. "You've fallen for me?"

"I'd say hook, line, and sinker, but in your case, it's more like you speared me."

A warm glow came over me, but that ignited as he finally gave in and let me have what I craved.

I would have slithered down to the concrete if Leo hadn't picked me up and dumped me on the hood. He propped my feet on the bumper, then slid my ass forward, squeaking along the paintwork.

I was too jellied to care.

A ripping of foil made me look up, and I saw Leo had shucked his shorts. Yup, his cock was just like the rest of him. Big, and oh so tasty. I caught sight of the condom in his hand.

"Is that from my bathroom?"

"Yeah."

Why did he have it with him? "You planned this?"

"I've been fantasising about it for weeks, ever since that night outside the summerhouse. Does that bother you?"

No, I guess it didn't. "Shut up and fuck me."

By the time Leo carried me upstairs, I had bruises everywhere—my ass where he'd pounded me into the metal, my legs where he'd held me down, and my lips where he'd bitten them. And I'd never felt so fucking happy in my life.

Boat? What boat?

Chapter 24

"SHIT, GORGEOUS. LOOK at the state of you."

I blinked a couple of times and found Leo lying on his side, looking down at me. At some point in the night I'd thrown the covers off, and now I was wrapped up only in him. The early morning light slanted through the window, highlighting the angles of his face, the deep blue of his eyes, the stubble speckled across his jaw. I ran the back of my hand along it, imagining that rough scratch between my legs. But he looked worried.

"What's wrong? Is it my hair?"

He pressed a soft kiss to my lips. "No, the rest of you."

I followed his gaze down my body. The bruises on my hips and arms had gone a delightful shade of purple. "Oops."

"I didn't mean to hurt you."

"You didn't. You made me feel alive. Believe me, I'd soon have stopped you if I hadn't been enjoying myself."

"I do believe you. But I'm not doing anything like that again until you've healed up."

I pouted, then cursed myself for it. "I want you."

His fingers whispered down my side and I rolled into him. "And you'll get me, but let's try something different. An experiment, if you like."

"What kind of experiment?"

Leo ghosted his lips over my shoulder, and while it didn't light me on fire, the tickle made me smile. "This morning, I'll give you sweet, and you can tell me which parts you like. We'll talk. Somewhere we'll find a level that makes you feel good without leaving marks all over your beautiful body."

"But I want you to feel good too. Won't it ruin things if we treat this like a science class?"

"As long as my cock's anywhere near you, I feel good. And..." He sucked in a breath, then turned my chin so our eyes met. "I want this to be a long-term thing. I'm not sure I'll ever get enough of you. If that's not what you're looking for, then please, tell me now."

"I want forever." If last night hadn't been enough for me to know, what he just said sealed it, and I blinked away the tears that threatened to embarrass me. "But once you find out more about me, you might think differently."

"Then tell me."

So I did. I couldn't look at him while I spoke, but he stroked my stomach as I faced away from him, never breaking the connection as I told him about my demented career and the honey traps. Not in any detail, but enough for him to realise I'd never been a good girl.

Then I waited.

"You said you were thinking of quitting?"

"I've already quit. I'm not going back to that. Something else, maybe. But not that."

Leo rolled me over and kissed my nose, a sweet gesture that made my heart swell so big I thought my ribcage would burst. "Then nothing changes. The past has shaped both of us, but we can't live in it. The future's ours, and we can make what we want from it."

"Make love?"

"How many condoms do we have left?"

"A handful. But I have contraceptive injections, and I got tested for everything after my last job."

"I'm clean, I swear."

"Then it's up to you."

He smiled in the way that made me melt, then shifted his hips and eased into me bare. That was a first for me too, and the connection that came from skin-on-skin meant he stole just a little bit more of my heart with every thrust.

What do you know? I could come from sweet sex. Not as hard, maybe, but Leo raining kisses on my face as he found his own release more than made up for that.

"We never did get dinner last night."

I didn't care. In fact, I only cared about one thing right now. Good grief, a decade of treating sex as a chore, and now I'd turned into a fucking nymphomaniac. "I'm not hungry. But I am sticky."

In accordance with Leo's insistence we experiment, he'd just shot a load over my breasts. The verdict? Slightly odd, but he enjoyed it so we'd do it again.

"Okay. Shower first, and then I'll make us breakfast."

He should have phrased that differently. He actually meant shower, then sex in the shower, then shower again. *Then* breakfast. But now I was sitting at the counter in front of a plate of waffles.

"You're a genius."

"They're not that difficult. All you need is a waffle iron, and I found one at the back of the cupboard while I was tidying."

"I'm gonna buy one when I get home. No, actually, I need to buy a home, and then I'm gonna get a waffle thingy."

"You don't have a home? So when we fly back to the US, where are you going?"

"I'll stay with a friend."

"A friend?"

Uh oh. More awkwardness. "You know ages ago I mentioned a woman? That I messed around with sometimes?"

"Yes."

That one word held a whole lot of worry. Shit. I forced a smile and did my best to reassure him. "It wasn't anything serious. Her husband thinks it's funny."

His eyes widened. "She's married?"

"Has been for years. Oh, hell, you think that's weird, don't you?"

"If we're going for honesty here, the thought of you and another woman, it's actually kinda...hot."

My turn to be surprised. "You don't mind?"

"If it's over and she's married, you're hardly gonna run off and leave me for her, are you?"

"Never, but she's a friend above all else. Like you," I added quietly.

Leo reached out and took my hands in his. "That's the most important thing. Lust is built on hormones, but love is built on friendship. I want you to be happy more than anything else."

A tear dripped down my nose and plopped onto my waffles. "I *am* happy." I wiped my cheek. "I don't know why I'm crying."

"Emotions are funny things. Sometimes you want them to go one way but they take you somewhere entirely different."

"How about Virginia?"

"That's where your friend lives?"

"Yeah. You can stay too if you want. She won't mind."

"Will she have enough space?"

"Plenty. Although it might not be as peaceful as here. She often has a bunch of other friends staying, and it sometimes gets noisy after the parties."

Leo burst out laughing. "I'm intrigued to meet her."

"I think you'll like her."

"Does she know all about you? I mean, your job?"

"We're in the same line of business."

Leo nodded as it dawned on him. "She's the person who's been helping us, isn't she? And she rented this house?"

"Yes."

"Then I owe her a hell of a thank you."

I shuffled my stool closer and wrapped my arms around him. After being alone for so long, I'd found my soulmate in the most unexpected place. I only wished the meeting hadn't been born out of tragedy, his sister's above all else.

Leo returned my hug, and for a few seconds, our world was perfect.

Then a scream broke the air.

CHAPTER 25

LEO SPRANG BACK and ran to the window. I followed quickly, chewing the bite of waffle I'd stuffed in my mouth. Hey, I didn't want to waste good food, okay?

On the rear deck of *Liquidity*, the secretary was wailing like a banshee. The only respite we got was when she paused to throw up over the edge. Too much gin? Or something else?

"Do you think Raul ate the sushi? I didn't even notice."

Leo grinned down at me. "I told you I'd take your mind off it."

"My mind's still floating around in the garage somewhere."

Leo turned his attention back to the window. On *Liquidity*, the captain was running along the outside gangway, and I accidentally snorted when his fancy hat flew off and landed in the water.

The shrieking carried on. "Help! Someone help!"

On impulse, I headed for the back door. No sign of Raul on deck meant he was likely inside, and I wanted to take a closer look at what was going on. I almost never got to see this bit, and the opportunity was too good to pass up. How much damage had a dozen slices of puffer fish liver done?

"Where are you going?"

"To help, of course."

"You're crazy."

"I know."

I hopped over the low wall that separated our dock from next door's, then repeated the move one more time until I reached *Liquidity*. Still no Raul.

"What's happened? Should I call someone?"

"We already have an ambulance coming," the captain said. "The owner collapsed in his bedroom."

I glanced across at the outside dining table, still with the scattered remains of lunch. Only a solitary uramaki roll remained, forlorn on the plate with a couple of pickled ginger slices next to it.

"I'm a nurse back home in the US. You want me to take a look?"

"If there's anything you can do..."

I followed the captain below decks, passing the deckhand on the way. He'd gone quite white, which I took as a good sign.

"How is he?" the captain asked.

Bodyguard number two looked up from his position on the floor next to Raul. "He has a pulse and his eyes are moving, but he can't speak properly."

Ah, stage two of tetrodotoxin poisoning, and something I'd only observed twice in practice. Fascinating. And with the dose he'd had, I gave him ten minutes.

But I was here to help, and help I would. "Do you have a first aid kit on board?"

"What do you need?"

"A thermometer if you have one."

I didn't need anything of the sort, just a few minutes alone with Raul. Although I couldn't deny the thought of ramming a thermometer up his ass held a certain appeal. But the pair didn't question me and dashed off.

Tetrodotoxin, one of the most potent neurotoxins known to man, had always intrigued me with its mechanism. In some cases, the victim remained conscious and lucid right up to death, albeit totally paralysed. I'd never seen that particular presentation myself. Would today be my lucky day?

I dropped to my knees beside the bastard who'd tried to end my life.

"Hey, sweetie. Did you miss me?"

The flash of recognition in his eyes would stay with me for the rest of my life. A memory right up there with my daddy's dying breath and my first million-dollar paycheque. A moment to treasure.

My darling ex tried to speak, but the other dude was right; he couldn't.

"At a loss for words, Raul? Shame. Still, I hope you enjoyed lunch. Fugu's a rare delicacy, and that one was real fresh. Caught it myself."

If looks could kill... But they couldn't.

"Fish got your tongue?"

Raul made a choking sound. Oh, I was enjoying this.

"What, honey? I didn't quite get that. Vivian's brother says hi as well, by the way. Sorry he couldn't be here, but he's packing for our flight home. We've had a lovely break. Sun, sea, sex. I should thank you for the introduction."

Raul's eyelids started to droop, and I picked up a limp wrist. His pulse beat in an erratic rhythm, dancing to its own brand of electro-pop. I was losing him.

Forgive me if I didn't shed a tear.

"Bye, sweetie. Enjoy hell. I'll probably meet you there someday, except I'll be in a deeper circle than you."

His eyes closed as the captain rushed in with the first aid kit.

"How's he doing? Do you know what's wrong with him?"

I injected a hint of panic into my voice, even though I felt at peace for the first time in years. "His heartbeat's all over the place, and I don't know what's the matter. How long will that ambulance be?"

The man glanced at his watch. "They said ten minutes, and that was five minutes ago."

Oh, good, he'd be long gone by the time they got him to the hospital.

"Do you have an on-board defibrillator?"

"Not that I know of."

Another plus point.

"I'm going to start CPR. Can you help with mouth-to-mouth?"

I didn't mind trying to crack a rib, but I was fucked if I was putting my lips near his grotty mouth again.

"Okay. How often do I breathe?"

"Every thirty chest compressions. I'll tell you when."

I sang softly to myself as I started on his chest —"Stayin' Alive" by the BeeGees. The perfect rhythm for CPR.

And ironic, because I was, and Raul wasn't.

After a brief discussion with Emmy, I decided to stay on an extra night or two with Leo. Leaving the Caymans so soon might arouse suspicion that wasn't otherwise there.

"It's worked out beautifully," she told me. "Vadim's still unconscious, but the oleander's cleared his system, and now they're speculating whether the same thing might have affected both of them."

That took all the heat off Leo at the gym, which could only be a good thing. And it meant the waters around my sushi delivery yesterday would most likely get muddied as well. Sure, yesterday's sushi may have killed Raul, but what about Vadim two days before? Oh, confusion reigned.

"It'll take them a day to do the autopsy and longer to get the results of toxicology tests," I said. "We'll fly home in a couple of days. Maybe fit in some sightseeing."

"Are you still coming here?"

"Yes. And Leo too."

"Hang on. Do you need one bedroom or two?"

"Er, one."

"For fuck's sake, Fia. Couldn't you have held out for two more days?"

And lose two days' worth of orgasms? Not a chance. "Look, I'll give you the fifty bucks myself."

"That's not the point. When did it happen?"

Emmy may have sounded pissed off, but I knew her, and in her own way, she was happy for me. "Last night."

"Before or after midnight? I'm talking Eastern Standard Time."

Same time zone as us. "Before."

"Dammit! Luther won again. He always wins. We're never gonna hear the end of this."

"If it helps, we were still going well into the next morning. Perhaps you could split it?"

"Oh, honey. He's good, then?"

I sighed, completely unable to help myself. Good didn't even begin to describe Leo. "He's everything." I paused. "And he knows about us. He doesn't mind."

"I think I might love him a little bit myself. I'll ask Mrs. Fairfax to get your room ready, and the champagne'll be waiting on ice."

"We couldn't have done this without you."

"I'll always be here for you. You know that."

"And I'll always be here for you too. Hoes before bros, right?"

Emmy hooted with laughter. "Too damn right. Now, sod off and enjoy yourselves."

CHAPTER 26

SIGHTSEEING, I TOLD Emmy. Sure. The only sights I saw were the sheets and every single inch of Leo's body. Oh, and the kitchen. He cooked me waffles every morning, then fucked me over the kitchen island. I developed a whole new appreciation for the cool smoothness of Italian marble.

But all good things came to an end, and three days later we really did pack our bags for the final time.

"I'll miss this house. It sure beats my old apartment," he said.

"Maybe we could pick out somewhere together when we get back?"

He locked up the door, and we moved to the stone bench at the edge of the driveway to wait for the taxi. The sweet fragrance of the oleander bushes drifted over to us, reminding me of happy times. When I got my own yard, I'd plant a whole row of them.

"You mean it?"

"We've been living together for the past couple of months. It seems silly to go back home and get two separate places."

He leaned in for a quick kiss. "Plus, I want to fall asleep next to you every night and wake up next to you every morning."

"I'm not sure about the falling asleep part. I've been

passing out from exhaustion."

"That works for me too. Although we'll have to ease up a bit when we get back because I'll need to get a job."

"Not right away, though. Can't we enjoy a month or two together and maybe a vacation? Then if you want to go back to work, you can."

"Fia, I have nothing. If we're gonna afford our own place, I'll need to start earning. We can't stay with your friend forever."

"She probably wouldn't notice if we did. She has, like, thirty bedrooms, and I think the guest house out the back is empty."

He stared at me. "Thirty bedrooms? Thirty? Three zero?"

"I haven't counted, but something like that. It's a big estate. I stay there whenever I want, and she honestly doesn't mind. Except one of her swimming pools has a fucking ice cream kiosk that makes me want to throw up every time I see it."

"Thirty bedrooms?"

"Split over two houses."

"What does she live in? A palace?"

"It's more of a replica stately home."

"Do we have to dress up for dinner? I don't even own a tie."

The idea of Emmy dressing up for dinner had me creased in half with laughter. "Nobody dresses up for dinner. There's nothing formal about the place at all, but if it makes you uncomfortable, we can stay someplace else."

"I'll start looking for a job when we get back. I'm in better shape now, and I figure I still have a few years left in me as a model. And I could do personal training on the side, although it'll take me a while to build up a client base from nothing."

"Leo, you don't have to." I laid a hand on his arm. "Do you know the going rate for a top-tier assassin?"

He flinched at the word, but I needed to be blunt. I was what I was.

"I've never thought about it."

"I got a million dollars when Raul died. And another two as a bonus for completing the project."

His eyes saucered. "Three million dollars?"

"It was deposited in my account yesterday."

Right after Mack sent off Raul's data. The cops in Atlanta were going to be shitting their pants or shouting hallelujah from the rooftops, depending on whether or not they happened to be on Raul's payroll.

"But that's your money, not mine. I don't like the idea of not paying my way."

"You did half the work on Raul. So you get half the money."

"I can't take that."

"You earned it."

"No, you did. I just helped out with some errands."

I'd worried he might say that. Leo was too damned self-deprecating for his own good. "Then let me buy us a house with it. Please."

"Okay."

I'd booked business class seats, but the girl on the ticket desk took one look at Leo and upgraded us to first, even if she did look down her nose at me while she did it.

"I've never flown anything but economy before," Leo whispered.

"It's just a bigger seat and better peanuts."

And a nice, fluffy blanket that Leo's hand could reach underneath and do bad things to me. I'd never had a flight go quite so fast before, or so pleasurably.

"Think we could join the mile-high club one day?" Leo murmured as I bit my tongue so hard it hurt. It was either that or scream and have everyone on the airplane stare at us.

"Not on one of these. We can borrow Emmy's jet for that."

"Emmy's your friend?"

"Oh. Yeah. I should probably have told you her name before now."

"And she has a jet? An actual plane?"

"Yeah. And everybody she knows has borrowed it to fuck in at some point or another. It's perfectly normal. Go up. Fly around a bit. Fuck. Land. The pilot's used to it."

He shook his head. "You live in a different world to me."

"No. *We* live in a different world to the one you lived in before. You're part of it now. Get used to the idea."

I'd been prepared to get a cab, but it didn't surprise me to find a limo driver waiting for us at the gate. Leo, of course, read the sign and looked behind to check there wasn't another Sofia following.

"It's for us. Get—"

"I know. Get used to it. I'm trying."

And his eyes nearly bugged out of his head when he saw the Riverley estate, the home Emmy shared with her husband. I couldn't blame him. The towering stone edifice with its row of gargoyles glowering down from the roofline was something to behold.

"It's... I know you said it was big, but..."

"I felt like that the first time I saw it too. But until now, it's the closest thing to a home I've ever had."

"Who are all those people?"

Emmy and her husband had walked out the front door, followed by Mack and her beau. Even the housekeeper came out to wave.

Then through the middle of them dashed a man wearing a neon pink onesie and cowboy boots.

"What the hell...?" Leo started.

I'd barely gotten out of the car when Bradley hit me full tilt. "Sofia! It's been so long! Three months! I redid your room when I heard you were bringing Leo home with you." Bradley gave him the once over, pausing at his ass. "Not bad. Anyhow, it's a shade darker now. More manly. I've put nine types of condom and three types of lube in the nightstand, there's champagne in an ice bucket, and the squirty cream and chocolate sauce are on the dressing table."

Chocolate sauce *and* squirty cream? He really spoiled me. "Bradley, I've missed you." I turned to Leo, who still looked utterly confused. "Leo, this is Bradley, Emmy's assistant. If you need anything, just ask him."

"Ooh, yes, sweet cheeks. Anything." Bradley's eyes dropped to Leo's ass again. "Anything at all."

I managed to extricate myself from Bradley's arms

and led Leo up the steps. "And this is Emmy."

He leaned down to kiss her on the cheek, the perfect gentleman, before I introduced him to everybody else. Then we picked up our bags and went inside.

"You joining us for dinner?" Emmy asked.

"We might be a few minutes late."

"I thought so. I'll see you tomorrow."

The next morning, I introduced Leo to the delights of Riverley's gym. His eyes gleamed, and I knew he'd be in there for hours.

"I'm gonna catch up with Emmy, okay?"

He pulled me hard against him, claiming me with his mouth. I understood why. He said he was okay with the Emmy thing, but there was still a hint of jealousy there. I'd need to be careful. And I also needed to get something off my chest.

"Leo, I love you."

A pause, then his face lit up as my words sunk in. Another second, and Leo picked me up and threw me into the air. *Threw me.* Then he caught me effortlessly and squeezed the life out of me like a steroid-addicted anaconda. No, on second thought, more of a boa constrictor. He kept the anaconda in his shorts.

"I love you too, gorgeous. And I meant it when I said you're the most amazing woman I've ever met."

"And I'm yours. Always."

"I know. Now, go and do whatever it is you do with Emmy."

I spun around on Emmy's husband's office chair while she sat behind her desk. Behind her, screens displayed the operating status of Blackwood and footage from various security cameras. But her attention was on the box of chocolates I'd bought for her at the airport.

"These are good." She held them out. "You want one?"

I popped a caramel into my mouth. "I should have picked up two boxes."

"One's enough. Toby's gonna kill me as it is." Toby was her nutritionist. "You managed to put Leo down for five minutes then?"

"He's in the gym, sorting out his six-pack. I hope he doesn't think we've snuck off somewhere to fuck."

Her laughter melded with mine. "Men have such dirty minds. I'll smear some lipstick over your face before you go."

I rolled my eyes. "Thanks. Remind me to do my buttons up wrong."

"I'm glad you've finally found someone. He seems nice."

"He looks after me."

The conference phone on the desk between us buzzed, right on time. Emmy reached over and pressed a button to answer it. The thing confused the hell out of me, and I usually ended up cutting people off instead.

"Snow?"

The hoarse voice of the Ice Cream Man came from the speaker. I'd never seen him without a cigarette in his hand, and how he'd survived to his sixties without succumbing to lung cancer never ceased to amaze me.

"I'm here."

"I need to congratulate you on a job well done."

"Thanks. The money said it all, really."

He laughed, then went into a coughing fit. "Still, we appreciated having you work through that list. Solved a lot of problems for us."

"Glad I helped. Did you want something in particular?"

"We were wondering if you'd be interested in trying a new flavour? Tutti frutti?"

"I can't. Sorry, but that was my last job."

Emmy smiled beside me, then squeezed my hand.

"The money's good on this one. Two million."

"It's not the cash. I've decided to get out of the business."

"A disappointment but not entirely unexpected. You've served us well over the years."

"I'd say it's been a pleasure, but I'd be lying."

He cackled again and coughed half a lung up. "You know where we are if you change your mind."

"I won't."

Emmy hung up, and I took a sip of my coffee. This was the start of a new day, of a new life, and what better way to start than with caffeine?

"I think you've made the right decision."

"With Leo in the picture now, it was the only one I could make. I want a future with him."

"What do you want for your wedding gift?"

I threw a pen at her, but the bitch caught it. "Don't talk about that. We've only been together a week."

"It'll happen. I'm thinking nursery furniture."

This time I scored a bullseye with a pad of sticky

notes. "And I've been thinking about what you said a while back. Do you have any openings at Blackwood?"

"For you, always."

"A lot of time's passed since we first met, and I think I'd like to be part of a team now."

"Then I'll see you in my office tomorrow." She winked. "Wear a short skirt and skimpy underwear. I'll bring my riding crop."

EPILOGUE

SOFIA SQUEALED AS Leo carried her over the threshold of their new home, and he couldn't help laughing.

"Never had you down as such a squealer, gorgeous."

"Neither did I. I don't know what's wrong with me lately."

Leo dipped his head and kissed her softly on the lips. "I do, because it's the same thing I'm suffering from." Another kiss, deeper this time. "Love."

"I'm not suffering from love; I'm enjoying every second of it, and speaking of seconds, we haven't been naked since this morning and I'm feeling rather empty, Mr. Moore."

With the extra strength gained from another month in the gym, Leo made short work of the stairs leading to the master bedroom. He hadn't seen it since last week, and Bradley had still been pointing at fabric swatches back then.

A quick nudge opened the door, and damn, Bradley had worked fast. The room looked great, although tonight, Leo only had eyes for the bed and the woman he wanted in it with him. And...what was that?

"Is that a gift?" Sofia asked.

"Sure looks that way."

"It's not from you?"

"I planned to give you something else."

He tossed her on the bed, and she crawled over to the box on the far side as he peeled off his shirt.

"It's from Emmy." Fia produced a knife from who-knows-where to slice off the ribbon, then tore into the purple tissue paper. "Oh, fucking hell, I don't believe her."

"Is that what I think it is?"

Sofia drew a torturous-looking implement from the box. It had a dark wooden handle with a silver snake coiling up it, topped with a red enamelled apple. Leather tails hung from the other end, and she trailed them over his naked chest.

"It is indeed." She reached back into the box and came out with a gold necklace, complete with jewel-studded tassels. "Can you put this on for me?"

He fumbled with the catch, all thumbs, until he'd fastened it around her neck.

"Beautiful, but not as beautiful as you." The two tassels hung between her breasts, and he rested one on his fingers. "Hang on... Are these nipple clamps?"

Sofia's smile grew wider. "Looks like it."

"And is that real gold?"

"Emmy would never buy fake."

Leo picked up the flogger and batted her ass with it. "I'm trying to work out how weird it is that your ex-lover bought us five-figure sex toys as a house warming gift."

"Forget weird and fuck me."

"With pleasure."

He shoved her back on the bed and straddled her, ripping her shirt off when she struggled underneath him. Those bruises he'd given her on their first night together still sickened him, and he'd never go that far again despite Sofia's urging, but he couldn't deny the way he got turned on when her skin flushed pink under his palm.

And sometimes, just sometimes, weird was good.

The sun shone in, landing across the bed in a thick swath of warmth and highlighting the golden streaks in Sofia's newly coloured locks. As usual, she'd wrapped herself around him in her sleep, and even though that often meant he woke up with a mouthful of hair, he wouldn't change it for anything.

He blew a few loose ends away and kissed her forehead, smiling as her eyes fluttered open.

"Good morning, Mr. Moore."

"Good morning, Miss Darke." She'd finally told him her real surname, although he couldn't help hoping she'd change it to match his. Not yet—she still had too many demons lurking inside her to take such a big step at the moment, but one day. One day, he wanted his ring on her finger.

"How's my ass this morning?" she asked.

He gave it a squeeze. "Pert."

"I meant, are there any marks?"

Leo raised his head a couple of inches from the pillow, his gaze lingering on the expanse of smooth, tanned skin leading to the most perfect bottom he'd ever seen.

"Nothing."

"Good. Then you can try harder after the party tonight."

"What about right now?"

She sat up, grinding down on his morning erection. "Right now, it's my turn to do the work."

The first meal Leo cooked in their new kitchen should have been breakfast, but it turned into lunch. Not that it mattered—they'd both taken the day off to spend it settling in before thirty guests arrived at seven for a housewarming party.

As Leo whipped up batter for waffles—Sofia's undisputed favourite—he looked out across the yard and wondered how the worst time of his life had turned into this. The place they'd chosen together was far more than he could ever have dreamed of—five bedrooms, a huge living room and highly specced kitchen, a two-car garage. No pool, as Sofia still hadn't regained her old love of water, but that didn't matter because the fitness centre they were building together had one being dug out right at that moment.

They'd discussed the future, and Leo had two options—go back to modelling until his body didn't meet with people's expectations anymore or open another gym. Sofia left the decision up to him, but he'd seen how much she valued her privacy, and he didn't want to draw attention to her or their life together by having any more pictures of himself splashed across the internet. Then she'd offered to invest in his new business, and it had made the decision easy. He'd built a profitable gym from nothing once, and this time he'd have a head start.

The only thing missing was Vivian. If he could

change one thing in his new life, it would be to have her there to enjoy it alongside him. Sofia meant the world to him, but nothing could replace his own flesh and blood.

He missed his sister, and he always would. But now he'd had this new life gifted to him, and it made him happier than he had a right to feel.

And he thought Sofia was happy too until she didn't come down for lunch.

"Fia, food's ready."

No answer. He tried again after he'd loaded the mixing bowl into the dishwasher, but silence reigned. Had she fallen asleep again? She'd certainly exerted herself earlier.

"Fia?" He climbed the stairs two at a time, worry pressing on his chest. "Where are you?"

Still nothing, but when he paused on the landing, he heard a quiet sobbing coming from the spare bedroom at the back of the house.

"What's wrong?"

She looked across from her position by the window, face streaked with tears. Oh, shit. Please say she wasn't having second thoughts? "Fia, what's happened?"

"It's nothing." She wiped her face with a sleeve. "Just these damned emotions keep getting the better of me."

"It's not nothing. Nothing wouldn't leave you crying alone in the middle of the day." He hesitated, afraid to ask his next question. "Have I done something wrong?"

"No. It's not you. I should be happy, today of all days."

"Then what is it? Have you been taking your pills?"

Sofia had confided about her mental health issues.

On the whole, she seemed to have them handled, but if she needed any support, Leo would be there for her. Always.

She walked to the bed and sank down onto the soft jade-green quilt Bradley had chosen. Leo perched next to her, getting more nervous by the second until she took his hand and pressed it to her lips.

"There are still things about me that you don't know."

"Then tell me. I promise I won't judge." Hadn't he proven that already? Surely nothing could be harder to stomach than finding out his girlfriend was, in fact, a paid assassin?

She gripped his hand tighter. "You remember when we first met, and you told me about Vivian and how she died?"

"Yes." He was hardly going to forget that moment or the panic attack afterwards.

"I agreed to help you because Raul tried to kill me too, but that wasn't the only reason. I also agreed because I understand the pain of losing a sibling."

Of all the possibilities flooding his mind, that hadn't been one of them. "Sweetheart, I'm so sorry. What happened? Actually, no, if you don't want to tell me that's okay too."

"Three days after my fourth birthday, my mom went to the store to pick up groceries, and she never came back. But she wasn't alone. She took my baby brother with her."

"Did he...? Are they...?"

"Dead? I don't know. I've been looking for them since I turned eighteen."

"And what have you found?"

"Nothing. Absolutely nothing. They just disappeared. The street I grew up on was bulldozed to make way for a mall, and nobody in town even admits to knowing my mother. All I know for sure is that she abandoned me."

"Maybe she didn't? Maybe your father..." Shit, he could hardly suggest the worst, could he?

"She planned it. Leaving, I mean. Just trust me on that—she left me behind." Fia shook with sobs again. "Why wasn't I good enough for her?"

Leo wrapped his arms around her. "Because she couldn't see what was right in front of her eyes. I'm not about to make the same mistake."

"I'm still scared you might come to your senses," she whispered.

"I already did that back in the Caymans when I fell for you."

Fia hugged him fiercely, and he returned the sentiment. "I love you," she whispered. "I've never told anybody else that."

"And I hope you never will unless we find your brother."

"We?"

"If there's anything I can do to help, I will."

"Blackwood's been looking for the past decade. If they can't find him, I doubt anyone can. Dammit, my life's finally going well, and I can't settle because he's missing."

"Well, the offer still stands." He gave her one last squeeze, then pulled back. "Do you want to cancel the party tonight?"

"No. This has been eating at me for years, but most of the time I can control it. Give me a few minutes, and

I'll be fine."

And to Leo's surprise, she was, at least on the surface. By the time the guests began showing up, she'd turned back into her usual self—a little sarcastic, smart as a whip, and beautiful as ever.

Leo was still getting to know Fia's friends and colleagues, but they were slowly becoming his friends too. Even Emmy's husband, who quite frankly scared the crap out of him. And now the man walked in his direction, holding out a magnum of chilled champagne.

"Happy housewarming."

Black didn't look happy, mainly because he never smiled.

"Thanks."

Leo took the bottle and put it in the refrigerator to keep cold. When he turned around, Emmy was waiting.

"How's Fia today?"

"Okay."

"Really?" Emmy clearly didn't believe him.

He sighed. "No. She was a bit upset earlier."

Of course, Emmy knew why. "Because of her brother?"

"Yes."

"Well, I've got some news that might cheer both of you up."

Fia walked in behind Emmy, sipping from a half-empty glass. "What news?"

"The police pulled a couple of Barone Senior's goons over for a broken taillight this morning."

"A broken taillight is news?"

"No, but the body they found in the trunk is. Guess Vadim finally outlived his usefulness."

"Vadim's dead?"

"He had a concrete block tied around his ankles, but he never quite made it as far as the river."

"Shame. Couldn't have happened to a nicer guy."

Leo caught the look on Fia's face when Emmy mentioned Barone Senior. Thoughtful. Calculating. Slightly worrying if he was honest. But then it vanished, replaced by a smile as Emmy brought some added cheer with her next piece of news.

"For a bonus, the Cayman Islands police force has closed the file on Raul. Word has it Daddy was so obnoxious to the coroner he did the bare minimum out of bloody-mindedness."

"So we're clear?" Leo asked. "No more toxicology tests?"

Emmy's smile matched Sofia's. Partners in crime, quite literally at times. "Better open that champagne, don't you think?"

Despite the audience, Leo couldn't resist pressing a soft kiss to Sofia's lips. "I think you're right."

She leaned into him, wrapping an arm around his waist. Although it was a tragedy that had sent him to the Caymans all those months ago, he couldn't help feeling happier today than he ever had in his life.

And then she returned his kiss. "We can celebrate properly later."

What's Next?

The Blackwood Elements series continues in *Carbon...*

Carbon

Meet me at midnight... When Augusta Fordham receives that message from an unknown admirer, the plot could have come straight from her favourite romance novel. Oh wait—it did.

Augusta is soon caught between wealthy doctor Gregory and a dark stranger who makes her pulse race as he indulges her fantasies. Will she choose comfort and security or take a leap into the unknown?

And more importantly, what secrets is Mr. Midnight hiding?

More details here:

www.elise-noble.com/carbon

And if you'd like to see more of Emmy, you can find her story in the Blackwood Security series, starting with *Pitch Black*.

Pitch Black

Even a Diamond can be shattered...

After the owner of a security company is murdered, his sharp-edged wife goes on the run. Forced to abandon everything she holds dear—her home, her friends, her job in special ops—she builds a new life for herself in England. As Ashlyn Hale, she meets Luke, a handsome local who makes her realise just how lonely she is.

Yet, even in the sleepy village of Lower Foxford, the dark side of life dogs Diamond's trail when the unthinkable strikes. Forced out of hiding, she races against time to save those she cares about. But is it too little, too late?

Warning
If you want sweetness and light and all things bright,
Diamond's not the girl for you.
She's got sass, she's got snark, and she's moody and dark,
As she does what a girl's got to do.

You can get Pitch Black for FREE here:

www.elise-noble.com/pitch-black

If you enjoyed *Lithium*, please consider leaving a review.

For an author, every review is incredibly important. Not only do they make us feel warm and fuzzy inside, readers consider them when making their decision whether or not to buy a book. Even a line saying you enjoyed the book or what your favourite part was helps a lot.

WANT TO STALK ME?

For updates on my new releases, giveaways, and
other random stuff, you can sign up for my newsletter
on my website:
www.elise-noble.com

Facebook:
www.facebook.com/EliseNobleAuthor

Twitter: @EliseANoble

Instagram: @elise_noble

If you're on Facebook, you may also like to join
Team Blackwood for exclusive giveaways, sneak
previews, and book-related chat. Be the first to find out
about new stories, and you might even see your name
or one of your ideas make it into print!

And if you'd like to read my books for FREE, you
can also find details of how to join my advance review
team.

Would you like to join Team Blackwood?

www.elise-noble.com/team-blackwood

END OF BOOK STUFF

When I wrote Oxygen, it was only supposed to be a novella, written because I felt kind of guilty for casting Akari as the bad guy in Forever Black through no fault of her own, and also because I fancied writing a book with more romance in it. But by the end of that story, I knew Sofia needed her own book.

When I first came up with the idea of the Horsemen for Gray is my Heart, Dan was supposed to be Snow, but as I wrote more of the Blackwood books I realised that didn't fit at all. But I still wanted my poisoner, because like Sofia, I've always been fascinated by the idea that an innocent-looking plant can have such a devastating effect on the human body. I mean, castor oil plants, oleander, foxgloves—they're all beautiful, and yet they give us ricin, oleandrin, and digitalin.

So, Sofia became Snow, a little twisted up inside and a lot deadly, driven by her past as we all are. And her brother? Well, more from him later...

As always, I couldn't have published this book alone. Huge thanks to my beta readers—Chandni, Ramona, Harka, Jeff, Renata, Helen, Terri, Lina, and Musi. Abi made me a lovely cover again—the knife was a wickedly good touch. Amanda, as always, made the editing as painless as possible, and thanks also to my awesome proof readers—John, Emma, and Dominique.

The next Elements book will be Carbon, and I'm not sure what I was thinking when I wrote that. It started off as a filthy novella then morphed into a thriller a third of the way through. I never like to be too predictable ;)

OTHER BOOKS BY ELISE NOBLE

The Blackwood Security Series
For the Love of Animals (Nate & Carmen - prequel)
Black is My Heart (Diamond & Snow - prequel)
Pitch Black
Into the Black
Forever Black
Gold Rush
Gray is My Heart
Neon (novella)
Out of the Blue
Ultraviolet
Glitter (novella)
Red Alert
White Hot
Sphere (novella)
The Scarlet Affair
Spirit (novella)
Quicksilver
The Girl with the Emerald Ring
Red After Dark
When the Shadows Fall
Pretties in Pink (TBA)

The Blackwood Elements Series
Oxygen

Lithium
Carbon
Rhodium
Platinum
Lead
Copper
Bronze
Nickel
Hydrogen (TBA)

The Blackwood UK Series
Joker in the Pack
Cherry on Top (novella)
Roses are Dead
Shallow Graves
Indigo Rain
Pass the Parcel (TBA)

Blackwood Casefiles
Stolen Hearts
Burning Love (TBA)

Blackstone House
Hard Lines (2021)
Hard Tide (TBA)

The Electi Series
Cursed
Spooked
Possessed
Demented
Judged (2021)

The Planes Series
A Vampire in Vegas (2021)

The Trouble Series
Trouble in Paradise
Nothing but Trouble
24 Hours of Trouble

Standalone
Life
Coco du Ciel (2021)
Twisted (short stories)
A Very Happy Christmas (novella)

Books with clean versions available (no swearing and no on-the-page sex)
Pitch Black
Into the Black
Forever Black
Gold Rush
Gray is My Heart

Audiobooks
Black is My Heart (Diamond & Snow - prequel)
Pitch Black
Into the Black
Forever Black
Gold Rush
Gray is My Heart

Printed in Great Britain
by Amazon

56258124R00135